Jay,

Love, Happy
Reading!

Jennifer Skinnell

MW00944955

1

One Sweet Development
©Copyright 2017 Jennifer Skinnell
All Rights Reserved
2nd Edition

Editing by Joanne LaRe Thompson

ONE SWEET DEVELOPMENT
By
Jennifer Skinnell

A Hope Springs Romance

Author Bio

Hello, I'm Jennifer Skinnell. I'm a quilter, blogger, the mother of two wonderful adult children, grandma to an adorable little boy, and wife of a wonderfully supportive husband. And now I can add author of One Sweet Development to that list! A life-long dream finally realized! I loved creating the town of Hope Springs with all its quirky characters of the Advice Quilting Bee. My pages may not be steamy, but I hope they make you laugh and fall in love with the residents of Hope Springs.

When I'm not writing, I'm quilting. For access to my world, check out my website www.jenniferskinnellquilting.com

Follow me on:
Facebook at Jennifer Skinnell Quilting
Instagram: @jenniferskinnell
Blog: www.theramblingquilter.wordpress.com
Twitter: @mommy66

Acknowledgements & Dedication

It takes a village to raise a child, and I feel it took a village to help me write this book! I'd like to thank my wonderful, loving, and supportive husband Mike, my children, Emily and Brian, and their spouses, Wade and Elizabeth, for believing in me and letting me live my dream. Marian, you were the perfect "Rosie", and I'm so glad I've gotten to know you better through this process. Thanks to my "unofficial" editors my daughter, Emily, and my friend, Heather, for being my guinea pigs. My friend, Faith, who, for 20 years, told me I could do this and lived up to her name, thank you for having faith in me. Thank you to Al Chesson for allowing me to use your beautiful J.H. Leary Building in Edenton, North Carolina as my inspiration for Rosie's Quilting Emporium. And to my new friend and editor, Joanne LaRe Thompson, thanks for taking a chance on an unknown!

I dedicate this book to my Aunt Jetta, who, as a teacher, inspired me and countless others to love reading and the English language. God took you from us too soon, but I was glad we had our impromptu breakfast so I could share with you my dream of writing this book.

To many, quilting is just putting two pieces of fabric together with a layer of batting between and making something to keep warm on cold winter nights. In colonial times, quilting Bees were gatherings of women around large quilting frames hand stitching the fabric pieces together while socializing and supporting one another.

Many quilters today have turned to machines in their individual sewing rooms to produce quilts faster, but losing the social aspect of quilting in the process. The ladies of Hope Springs have embraced the art of hand quilting, and as a result socializing, supporting and advising each other is a large part of their weekly gatherings. They have come to be known as the Advice Quilting Bee.

The Ladies of the Advice Quilting Bee

Rosie Macintire – Matriarch and Founder of the Advice Quilting Bee, owner of Rosie's Quilting Emporium widowed, 2 children - Robert, the Hope Springs Bank President, and Ramona, deceased

MaryAnn Macintire – Married Rosie's son, Robert; works at Rosie's Quilting Emporium

Missy Macintire – MaryAnn's daughter, works at Everything's New Again Boutique

Chandler Bradford – Single, owner of Sweet Stuff Bakery

Myrtle Freeman – Rosie's best friend and fellow quilter, unofficial president of the Little Old Lady Network, 6 grown children including Ben, the Hope Springs Fire Chief

Candy Freeman – Married to Myrtle's son, Ben; works part-time at Rosie's

Luann Freeman – Candy's daughter, college senior who works at the bakery during the summer

Fran Mayfield – Owner of Hope Springs Mercantile & Ice Cream Shop, member of the Little Old Lady Network, divorced, no children

Macy Greenburg – Chandler's best friend and neighbor, nurse at the Hope Springs Medical Center

Hillary Smith – Owner of Everything's New Again Boutique, married to Jack, 2 children

Andrea Porter – Owner of Hope Springs Diner, widowed, no children

The Town of Hope Springs

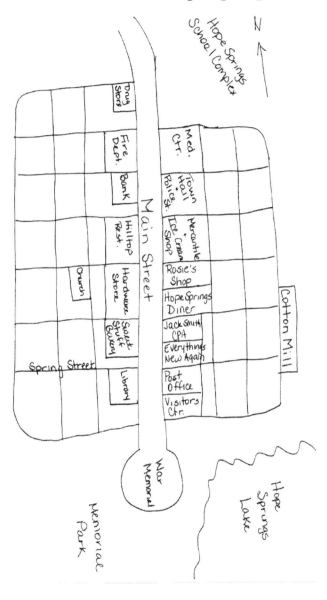

Prologue

I've had it! Thought Chandler Bradford as she got in her car and banged her hand against the steering wheel. She had put a lot of time and effort into this relationship, and Victor Confer didn't seem to care one bit. Why couldn't he see that it was all one-sided? He never drove the hour it took to get to Hope Springs to see her, but she was expected to attend every function at his art gallery in the city.

Of course, he also expected her bakery, Sweet Stuff, to supply all the sweets he needed for said functions at no cost. His reasoning was that she was getting a lot of "free" publicity. Her argument was that the time alone it took to bake and deliver these sweets was worth a lot more than the small amount of business she was gleaning from the publicity, let alone the cost of ingredients for his fancy food. Her usual small-town cuisine wasn't good enough for his clientele.

On top of that, his business partner hinted that their relationship may be more than just business. It was then that Chandler decided it was time to end it, whatever it was. She couldn't trust that someone from the city would ever want to live in her small town, and she certainly didn't want to move here. Chandler had lived in Hope Springs all her life. She loved the slower pace, peace, and tranquility that her small town had to offer. Just driving in the city drove her nuts! She couldn't imagine living here permanently. Plus, her feet were killing her in her four-inch heels. In her home town, she could wear sneakers and no one cared.

Chandler started her SUV and pulled out into the bustling traffic. She needed to go home, but what she really needed was to calm her frayed nerves before she tackled the drive. She spotted a pub up the street with valet parking, and decided to take a chance that it would be a quiet atmosphere where she could just sit and collect herself.

After giving the valet her keys and receiving her ticket, Chandler walked inside. The place wasn't overly packed, but it wasn't quiet either. It was more like a high-class sports bar. There were linen tablecloths with candles in the center, but also flat screen televisions showing various sporting events. Definitely not your average sports bar.

Chandler took a seat at a small table by a window. On one side she had a view of the busy sidewalk and street beyond, and on the other a television showing a baseball game featuring the Crusaders. Chandler wasn't a huge sports fan, but she did love the local baseball team; she had even gone to a few games.

The waiter stopped by Chandler's table, took her order for a glass of Merlot, and asked if she would like anything to go with it. It was then that Chandler realized how hungry she was, having not eaten anything at the gallery. After looking at a menu, she ordered a grilled chicken platter, which consisted of a grilled chicken breast, baked potato, and vegetable medley. It seemed like the most calorie-conscious thing on the menu.

As Chandler sat there sipping her wine, she felt herself starting to calm down. She noticed a group of men a few tables away watching the baseball game intently. Just then someone on the screen hit a home run, and they all erupted into cheering and high fives. Unfortunately, from her vantage point, she couldn't make out the score of the game.

"Hey, what's the score?" she asked the group.

They all turned and looked at her. "Five to four, Crusaders," one of the men answered.

"Thanks, I can't quite see it from here," Chandler replied, looking around the group toward the television.

Peter Frederick had noticed the slender girl with long auburn hair walk in during the seventh inning. She seemed a bit frazzled and didn't appear to notice anyone at all as she sat down at a table behind them. He thought she was a bit overdressed for Crandy's Pub, even though most of the clientele came from straight from their office jobs. This woman, however, wore an elegant emerald green dress hemmed just above the knee, with spiked heels. The color of the dress matched her eyes perfectly. He doubted she wore that to any job around here, at least not a legal one, and she didn't appear to be that type.

"What brings you into Crandy's, all dressed up?" Peter asked. For some reason he was curious.

Chandler looked around at the rest of the patrons. "Guess I am a little overdressed," she commented, with half a smile before lifting her glass to take a sip of wine.

"A little bit," he said, smiling. "Don't get me wrong, you look great, but you also look like you belong at a gallery opening, not a sports bar."

Chandler almost choked on her wine. "As a matter of fact, that's where I was before I came here."

"They didn't serve wine there?" Peter indicated toward her beverage.

"Not the kind I like," Chandler stated with a note of sarcasm. A bit of a strange conversation to be having, but the handsome man asking her questions at least took her mind off the idiot she'd just broken up with down the street.

"You like the Crusaders?" Peter asked, sensing something happened at the gallery that she would rather not talk about.

Chandler was grateful for the change in subject. "I'm not a huge sports fan, but I do love the Crusaders. I think it's because baseball is slower and easier for me to follow." Many times, Chandler had put a game on the radio at her bakery while she was working late into the evening finishing up a cake for a customer. Something about the way the game was called on the radio kept her hands steady.

"Not into football, basketball, or hockey, huh," stated Peter. He loved all sports, all the time.

"I enjoy watching them as well," she answered. "But when I'm working, I like listening to baseball on the radio."

"What kind of work do you do that allows you to listen to a game?" Peter asked.

Chandler wasn't sure how much she should tell a complete stranger, so she just kept it simple, "I'm a baker. I need steady hands when I'm decorating."

"Oh, that makes sense," he said, just as her dinner arrived. "Well, I'll let you eat in peace. Go Crusaders!"

"Go Crusaders!" she replied, raising her fist in the air. Chandler was glad he let the conversation drop. She just wanted to finish her dinner and get back to Hope Springs; she was done with the city and especially the men who lived there. Even though there weren't a lot of eligible men in Hope Springs, surely, she would find the right one someday. In the meantime, she had a bakery to run.

Chapter 1

Rosie Macintire woke to a bright June sun streaming through her bedroom window. As she stretched her arms over her head sending a silent thanks to the Lord for another day, Rosie knew it was the Lord who got her to the age of eighty-three. She got out of bed and walked to her closet, noting that for someone her age, she had little to complain about, health-wise. She didn't have many aches or pains and was of sound mind and body, as folks liked to say. Rosie took great care in making sure she ate properly, got the rest she needed, and her morning exercise was walking to her shop.

As Rosie surveyed the outfits in her closet, she remembered the weatherman saying it would be hot and sunny. She chose a pair of lavender capris and a cotton floral coordinating top; a pair of comfortable sneakers completed the ensemble. She applied a little blush on her cheeks, lipstick on her lips, and fluffed her short, curly, silver-white hair. As she finished getting ready, Rosie looked in her full-length mirror. *Not bad for someone my age*, she thought.

Rosie made her way down the center hall staircase of her two-story, Victorian home and into her kitchen. After having her breakfast of cereal and a cup of hot coffee, she walked out the front door onto the veranda. She stopped, as she always did, to secure the door and turned to face the day. Looking around at all the flowering plants lining her veranda and the front sidewalk, Rosie inhaled deeply the scent of so many flowers. She loved this time of year when everything was blooming and you could just smell the scent of new growth in the air. Her family had been taking care of these gardens for generations and she was so proud to have been able to keep it looking just as beautiful.

Rosie began her walk from her home in the historic district toward the center of Hope Springs. Even though her house was only two blocks from her shop, she always headed north on one of the side streets and made her way toward the fire station and medical center across the street. Especially in beautiful weather, Rosie liked adding more distance to her commute. She never got tired of seeing the history in the buildings lining Main Street; it was like stepping back in time. Main Street was only about seven blocks long and was the dividing line between the historic and the industrial districts.

Hope Springs was proud to have such a rich history. The heart of the town was full of homes and businesses built in the late 1700s and early 1800s. The outlying farms were well known for producing tobacco and cotton as their main cash crops. Fortunately, many of the structures sustained minimal damage during the Civil War. Hope Springs, however, was like many towns which lost a number of men to the war. At the south end of Main Street, a War Memorial had been erected in their honor. The names of some of Rosie's ancestors were etched in the stone surrounding it.

The historic district on one side of Main Street featured stately two-story homes with grand staircases and wide verandas, perfect for the social gatherings of the town's upper crust. On the other side in the industrial district, the streets were lined with small, one story, two- and three-bedroom cottages that used to house the Cotton Mill workers and their families.

The fairly new Hope Springs school complex, complete with new athletic fields for every sport imaginable, was on the north end of Main Street. Across the street, they had just completed the town's first chain drug store. From that point on south, for the most part the buildings aged like fine wine.

The industrial district was primarily defined by the Cotton Mill. The mill was the main employer in Hope Springs until it closed a couple of decades earlier. As a result, much of the town's businesses also packed up and left. The two-story building still stood today; however, it was in need of some tender loving care. One by one, the surrounding cottages were being restored by new owners who were drawn to Hope Springs from the city because of its small-town feel.

The same could be said of the historic district mansions on Rosie's side of Main Street. Once home to the wealthy business owners and their families, many were left vacant when the businesses left Hope Springs. These stately homes were now being returned to their former glory by folks moving from the city for a slower pace of life. Rosie loved seeing the eclectic mix of residents breathing new life into the heart of Hope Springs. One thing was certainly true about the current residents of Hope Springs—they loved the history of the town and would do anything to return it to its former glory. Much to Rosie's delight, the town was slowly coming back to life.

As she continued her walk down Main Street, toward the Hope Springs Medical Center, Rosie reflected on her life in this small town. She met her husband, Charles, many years earlier when he came to work at the Hope Springs Bank. Rosie and her friends would walk past the bank on their way to the library, and Charles would ultimately be standing by the door as they passed. One day he finally spoke to her and asked if he might stop by her house sometime. Rosie had just turned eighteen and was getting ready to go to college. Her father was the bank president, he approved wholeheartedly of Charles courting her. Charles came by Rosie's house the next day, and just about every day after that, until she left to go to college. Five years after they met, they were married, and spent fifty-four wonderful years together. There had certainly been a lot of changes to the town in that time.

"Good morning, Macy," Rosie called out as she walked by the Medical Center. "Going in to work early today, I see." Macy Greenburg was one of the newer residents in Hope Springs.

"Yes, Rosie, I am," Macy replied, sliding her sunglasses on top of her wavy, long, red hair. "I really love working for Dr. Howard. He's so good with the patients. This week there seems to be something going around, so we've been really busy."

"Believe it or not, I grew up with Dr. Howard. He was always interested in medicine, and I knew he would end up a doctor one day," said Rosie. "I was so happy to hear he was going to open his practice here in Hope Springs when he finished medical school. It's hard to believe he'll be retiring soon."

"I know," said Macy. "I sure hope we get another doctor like him." Macy had just come from a practice in the city, and Rosie knew she liked the small-town doctor much better. She thought there was a story behind Macy's departure from the city practice, but Macy hadn't said anything…yet. Rosie had been around long enough to know that eventually Macy would open up. She also knew not to pry.

"Will we see you tonight?" Rosie asked to change the subject, referring to their weekly Advice Quilting Bee that was held at her shop, Rosie's Quilting Emporium.

"Absolutely, I just love getting together on Thursday nights. I may not know how to quilt very well, but I really enjoy visiting with everyone," Macy said, using her hand to shield her blue eyes from the morning sun.

"I'm so glad you are enjoying it, dear," Rosie said, smiling. "Well, I'll let you get on with your day. Hopefully it won't be as busy as yesterday. We'll see you tonight."

"Have a wonderful day, Rosie," Macy said as she went into the building.

"Good morning, Rosie," yelled Ben Freeman from the Hope Springs Firehouse across the street.

Good morning to you, too, Ben," Rosie said as she waved. "How is everything at the firehouse?"

"Quiet this morning," Ben said, in a deep voice with a thick southern accent. "Are you ladies meeting tonight?"

"Yes, we are."

"Darn, then that means we're on our own for dinner here," Ben said, smiling. Ben was Rosie's best friend, Myrtle's son and had grown up with Rosie's own son, Robert. Together, Ben and his wife, Candy, had a daughter, Luann, who had just finished her junior year in college. While Rosie's son has grown up to be the town banker, Ben had always wanted to be the fire chief of Hope Springs.

Rosie smiled. "I'm afraid so. I'm sure you'll cook up something delicious to feed the guys. It's wonderful that Andrea gives you all the leftover food from the diner, though." Andrea Porter and her husband had taken ownership of the Hope Springs Diner three years earlier, after moving from the city. Unfortunately, her husband passed away from cancer a little over a year ago. He had been a member of the Hope Springs Volunteer Fire Department, and Andrea took it upon herself to make sure the men and women who served the community were taken care of.

"We really appreciate it, that's for sure," said Ben.

"I know you do, Ben. And I know Andrea enjoys being able to feed you all," Rosie answered back. "Have a great, uneventful day, Ben," she said, waving as she continued on toward her shop.

Ben smiled and waved back, yelling, "You have a great day too, Rosie."

Chapter 2

As Rosie continued down the street, she looked over at the Hope Springs Community Bank building next to the firehouse. The building dated back to the turn of the twentieth century and had gone through some additions over the years to add the conveniences of the twenty-first century, including an ATM and drive-up window. Many historical features like the original walk-in safe remained, however. That was what Rosie loved about Hope Springs. Even though businesses were adapting to keep up with the changing times, the original architecture remained intact.

Rosie looked up at the Town Hall as she walked by. The town offices and police station were in this building, as were several law offices. Fortunately, she thought, the police were mostly for show, and the law offices were mostly for wills and probate. Definitely not much crime took place in Hope Springs and that suited Rosie just fine.

As she walked past Hope Springs Mercantile, Fran Mayfield was just opening the door.

"Good morning, Fran," said Rosie. "It's a beautiful day."

"Well, hello, Rosie," Fran greeted her as she stepped outside and began cleaning the first of three wrought iron table and chair sets that were in front of the store. While Rosie was more conservative in her dress, Fran was more a child of the sixties. On this day she wore a flowery, peasant top over a long, ruffle-bottomed, cotton, striped skirt. Her pink painted toe nails peeked out from her sandals. She chose to put her long, graying hair in a ponytail with a ribbon around it, and her tortoise shell glasses were secured around her neck with a beaded chain.

"It sure is," Fran continued. "I almost hate to stay inside, but the store won't run itself! I just made a pot of coffee. Care to join me?"

Rosie looked at her watch, "I think I have time for a cup. Shall we sit out here?" she asked, motioning to the freshly cleaned chairs that were still shaded by the building. "It's going to be a warm one, but it's shady on this side of the street."

"Sounds like a great idea," Fran said. "You take it black, right?"

"Yes," Rosie confirmed. "Can I give you a hand?"

"Nope, you have a seat and I'll be right back," Fran answered, as she went back into the store.

While Fran went inside to get the coffee, Rosie took a minute to look around. She loved how the town garden club had taken time to install small planters in front of the shops between the sidewalk and street curbs. They were overflowing with colorful petunias, begonias, violets and ivy, and really helped with the small-town feel. The black wrought iron benches placed along the sidewalk invited folks to sit, relax, and enjoy the view.

"Here we are," said Fran, carrying out two cups of coffee and placing one on the table in front of Rosie before sitting down with her own cup. She breathed in deeply and looked around. "I just love the flowers in front of our shops, don't you?" she commented, adjusting her top over her lap.

"I was just thinking that very same thing," said Rosie taking a sip of the hot coffee. "Ahhh, this is wonderful," she said, smiling. "It's so nice to see everyone taking such pride in our town and making it more welcoming for visitors."

Just then, a little convertible pulled up in front of the town hall, with a woman neither had seen before behind the wheel. Rosie and Fran watched as the young woman checked her makeup in the visor mirror and smoothed her long, blonde hair. Blowing herself a kiss in the reflection, she opened the door and got out of the vehicle, straightening her navy suit skirt. She tucked in her white, sleeveless blouse, and then put on the matching jacket, before picking up her briefcase from the back seat and marching into the courthouse on very high heels.

"Speaking of visitors, I wonder who that is," said Fran, curiously.

"Not sure, but she seemed a little underdressed, if you ask me," said Rosie.

"What do you mean? She was fully dressed," said Fran curiously.

"Must be my age, but I think she forgot part of her skirt at home. It barely covered anything. And with those high heels, she looked like she was just a pair of legs and a head." She didn't consider herself to be that prim and proper, but she felt a lady should be fully covered when she left the house.

"Ladies definitely dress differently than when we were that age," Fran said, laughing. "I'm not sure I could have pulled off that look! However, she was definitely secure in herself. Did you see her blow a kiss to herself in the mirror?" she asked, almost in disbelief.

"Yes, I did," smiled Rosie. "Guess we'll find out soon enough who she is and what she's up to. Things don't stay a secret for long in this town."

Fran laughed. "You're right about that," she answered, taking a sip of her coffee.

Rosie finished the last of her coffee and placed her cup on the table. "Well, I guess I'd better get over to my shop and get the day started. Are you coming tonight?" Rosie asked as she got up from her chair.

"Wouldn't miss it," said Fran. "Have a great day."

"You have a great day as well. And thanks for the coffee," Rosie said, handing her empty cup to Fran.

Rosie walked next door to her own shop, Rosie's Quilting Emporium. Located on the first floor of a building constructed just before the Civil War, it looked like it was made to house a quilt shop. The architectural design on the front of the building was made of wood cut in the shape of rectangles, squares set on point, and even scallops framing the windows. The colorful red, white, and blue paint gave the appearance of a quilt draping the façade.

As Rosie was putting her key into the front door lock, Andrea Porter came out of the diner next door. "Good morning, Andrea," said Rosie with a smile. "Love the leopard print top you're wearing today." Andrea rarely wore prints, but if she did most likely it would be some type of animal print.

"Good morning, Rosie," Andrea said, as she was putting out the easel announcing the day's special. "Thanks. Today seemed like a leopard print kind of day," she answered, straightening the knit top over her denim capris. "I'm looking forward to seeing everyone tonight. I made extra cornbread today so there would be some left over."

"Wonderful. I just saw Ben a little while ago and he wasn't too happy it was Thursday. He said he'd have to figure out what to fix the guys for tonight," Rosie said with a smile.

"I know they really appreciate everything I'm able to give them at the end of the day, and I'm happy to do it. Don't want anything to go to waste," Andrea said, brushing her curly, brown hair away from her face. "I think it's going to be a warm one, today," she said, fanning her face. "Either that or I'm starting to have hot flashes at the age of forty-five!"

Rosie laughed, "I think you're probably too young for that, Andrea. Let's just go with a hot day."

As they were standing there chatting, the woman Rosie and Fran had seen earlier came back out of the town hall with Mayor Thompson. They were laughing, and his cheeks seemed a little flushed. "Wonder what that's all about?" asked Andrea, curious who the woman was.

"Not sure who she is," Rosie answered, "but Fran and I saw her go in a little while ago. Obviously she had some kind of business with the mayor."

"Do you think his wife knows about this business?" asked Andrea, jokingly.

"Surely you don't think a young, pretty girl like her has something going on with our pudgy, old mayor?" asked Rosie, a little shocked Andrea would suggest such a thing. "One would think she would have better taste and he would have more decorum."

"You have a point there," Andrea said, laughing. "But she does seem out of place in Hope Springs."

"Well, as I told Fran, we'll know soon enough. Nothing stays a secret too long in Hope Springs," Rosie repeated before unlocking the door to her shop.

"That's true. Have a great day and I'll see you tonight," said Andrea, heading back into the diner.

"You too, dear," said Rosie, opening the door and looking back at toward the mayor and the woman. She watched as the woman got in her car and drove off. Rosie saw the mayor looked around, giving her an embarrassed wave, before rushing back into the courthouse. Rosie waved back and went inside her shop.

Chapter 3

Rosie looked around and felt a sense of pride at being able to make Rosie's Quilting Emporium a modern quilt shop while keeping the integrity of the history intact. The gleaming, original hardwood floors contained wear marks from years of customers. Rosie had used the original shelving units that lined the walls to display row upon row of colorful quilting fabrics. To the left of the main aisle, completed samples for upcoming classes were displayed above the shelves housing batik fabrics, patterns, and notions. The cutting table and checkout were in front of this wall.

Across the aisle, the wall of shelves on the right side of the store was filled with geometric, solid, and textured fabrics of every color imaginable, along with many other types of coordinating fabrics one might need to create the perfect quilt. In front of that were shorter rows of specialty fabrics, including florals, seasonal, novelty, holiday, and designer collections. The window displays housed the newest fabric lines and ways to use them. Across the back of the store was a small office and large storage room.

The crown jewel, however, was the large quilting frame between the main store and office/storage area. In an age where everything was done on larger quilting machines, Rosie preferred to do what things she could the old-fashioned way. She had a frame large enough for a king-size quilt, which she had set up all the time. Rosie loved teaching the lost art of hand quilting, which was how the Advice Quilting Bee came to be in existence. The original intent was to get a group of ladies around the frame to help finish a quilt someone had pieced for a specific charity. Over the years, however, it evolved into so much more.

The group consisted of a mix of women from their early twenties to early eighties. Throughout the years the older ladies had taken it upon themselves to impart their knowledge of many different subjects on the younger members of the group. As time passed, the group had become known around town for helping to solve all sorts of problems by giving their advice; thus became the name of the group, the Advice Quilting Bee. Some nights, ladies came to the group strictly looking for advice, with no intention of quilting at all. Not only did they get their advice, they usually ended up picking up a needle and thread and helping with the quilt in progress. Some even returned week after week, having caught the quilting bug, or just because they enjoyed the company of the other ladies in the group. Hearing the town gossip was also a bonus.

Much to Rosie's delight, the ladies of the Advice Quilting Bee filed into the back of Rosie's Quilting Emporium every Thursday evening. She was still going strong, but meeting with her friends put an extra pep in her step at the end of each week. Each lady had her specific chair, where she lovingly stitched her section of the current quilt on the frame. There were five chairs on each of the long sides with one chair at each end for anyone who dropped by.

Rosie was so proud of the accomplishments of each and every woman in the group. Nearly all of the ladies either owned or managed one of the small businesses in town. For this reason, Rosie scheduled the Advice Quilting Bee for Thursday evenings instead of during the workday. This seemed to be the best evening of the week, as to not conflict with various other meetings and events the women attended. Plus, it gave them a little respite from their hectic schedules before the weekend.

Rosie got to work opening the shop. As she flipped the light switches on, she could hear the hum of the florescent bulbs warming up. She knew that soon her daughter-in-law, MaryAnn, would be arriving to get the computerized cash register going, so she went to the back and started the coffee that was always ready for anyone who wanted it. Rosie knew that many new shops didn't offer refreshments to their customers, but she figured some traditions were worth keeping around. Plus, many of her customers were older and brought their husbands with them. She had a "patient husband area" for them to drink their coffee while their wives shopped. Rosie had learned long ago that if the husband was occupied, he couldn't talk his wife out of spending money in her shop!

As Rosie came back to the front, MaryAnn Macintire was letting herself in the front door. "Good Morning, Rosie," MaryAnn said, walking over and placing a box containing a crockpot full of her Mexican tortilla soup on the counter. "Boy, that is one heavy crockpot," she commented, brushing back her dark brown bob-cut hair, which had gotten blown in the breeze, and straightening her light pink top over her floral skirt.

"Good morning," Rosie answered, giving her daughter-in-law a hug. "How is everything at your house today?"

"Robert was up and at 'em early this morning. He said something about needing to get to the bank before some meeting with the mayor." MaryAnn had married Rosie's son, Robert, twenty-seven years earlier, and the two had given Rosie a wonderful granddaughter, Missy. Robert had carried on the family tradition of becoming the bank president of Hope Springs Community Bank, like his grandfather before him.

"Well, that's interesting," Rosie said with a sly smile. She placed her hand on MaryAnn's petite shoulder, "When you see him at lunchtime, please ask him if he knows anything about the pretty, young woman who met with Mayor Thompson."

MaryAnn's mouth dropped open. "Mayor Thompson met with a pretty, young woman already this morning?" Just the thought of pudgy Mayor Thompson being with anyone, let alone a pretty, young woman caused MaryAnn to shiver. "You don't think there is anything going on, do you?" she asked, skeptically.

"Well, Fran and I saw her go into the town hall and then about a half an hour later, Andrea and I saw her and the mayor come back out," Rosie explained. "You know that I'm usually the last person to gossip, I'm just telling you what I saw."

"That's true," said MaryAnn, knowing that gossip was something Rosie rarely did. "I'll definitely see if I can find out what that was about."

Rosie figured she didn't have to say anything more because MaryAnn would get the scoop soon enough.

MaryAnn carried her crockpot to the back counter and plugged it in. *Wouldn't that be quite the scandal,* she thought, *but honestly, the mayor and a young woman?* She got the chills again just thinking about it.

Chapter 4

The rest of the day was pretty much a blur. Rosie and MaryAnn were busy most of the day, and by about 4:00 p.m., both were ready for a break. Luckily, that was about the time the last customer left. MaryAnn encouraged Rosie to go to the back office and rest for a while before everyone started arriving around 6:00 p.m. At eighty-three, she sometimes needed to lie down if the day had been busy, so Robert had put a couch in the back office for her.

MaryAnn spent the time straightening up the shelves and closing out the cash register. Around 5:45 p.m., Rosie came out of the office looking more rested than when she went in.

"MaryAnn, is everything ready for our dinner tonight?" Rosie asked. She knew that most of the ladies came straight from work and wouldn't have time to eat dinner elsewhere, so there was always something prepared.

"Yes, Rosie, we're all set," MaryAnn answered, giving her a thumbs up sign. "I love Thursday night for so many reasons, but not having to cook at home is definitely near the top of the list," she said with a big smile.

"But you provided the main course tonight," Rosie reminded her.

MaryAnn shrugged her shoulders. "Somehow when you're just throwing all the ingredients in the slow cooker and turning it on, it doesn't feel like cooking."

"Something sure smells good in here," Fran called as she came in the front door and removed her turquoise-colored sunglasses. "What's on the menu tonight?"

"Mexican tortilla soup," MaryAnn replied as she finished up the closing duties. "Andrea told Rosie this morning she had cornbread to contribute."

As if on cue, the door opened and Andrea walked in carrying a big tray containing not only the cornbread, but also some leftover macaroni and potato salads. "Hi ladies!" she greeted her friends as she put the heavy tray down on the counter.

"Hi. Was the diner busy today?" Fran asked as she surveyed the contents on the tray.

"It really was, for a Thursday," Andrea answered. "Not sure what the occasion was, but I hope it continues. How was business at the mercantile?"

"I couldn't believe how busy we were. You would think a tour bus showed up or something!" Fran had owned the Hope Springs Mercantile and Ice Cream Shop for years, and had definitely seen the highs and lows in the town.

Hillary Smith and Chandler Bradford came in next. "Hey, Fran, I have some new things in at the shop I think would look great on you," Hillary directed at Fran. Hillary owned Everything's New Again Boutique, the local consignment shop. She always gave the girls a heads-up if she saw something come in she thought was perfect for them. "Stop in tomorrow and take a look."

"I think I might just do that," Fran said excitedly. "I'm all for adding to my wardrobe, and at a great price, too!"

"Where do you want this, MaryAnn?" Chandler asked, carrying a tray loaded with an assortment of baked goods from her Sweet Stuff Bakery.

"Over here will be great, Chandler," MaryAnn answered, clearing a place on the counter for the large tray.

"Ladies, I hope you left your calorie counters at home," Chandler said with a laugh as she placed the tray next to the other items on the counter. "Even though I was swamped with customers today, I still managed to have some leftovers. Does anyone know why there were so many people in town?" She brushed some leftover flour dust off her navy Sweet Stuff Bakery t-shirt. "I really should have gone home and changed. I have remnants of the bakery all over me," she laughed.

"Oh, please," remarked MaryAnn, "you look fabulous no matter what you're wearing."

"Very true," agreed Hillary, laughing. "You're wearing a floury t-shirt and frosting-covered jeans and you pull it off like it's the latest fashion craze. If that were me, I'd just look like I was wearing dirty clothes!"

"You're both too kind," Chandler said, chuckling, "but of course, it's not like I'm here to catch a man or anything." She took her ponytail holder out of her hair and finger-brushed it. Then she pulled it back, and redid the ponytail. "Okay, now I feel ready to go," she laughed.

Hillary mentioned that she overheard one of the ladies who ventured into her shop say there was a group in town scouting out potential development possibilities. "Apparently the town council is looking into a revitalization project and has been courting developers."

"You know, there was one woman who came into the bakery asking if she could take pictures. I just figured she was a tourist interested in the old architecture of the building, so I said she could. I wonder what she was really up to?" asked Chandler, concerned. She knew the building dated back to the Civil War and was in need of some love, but the landlord told her the budget couldn't handle it right then. It unnerved her a little that someone might be looking into development projects in her small town.

"I heard there was a group having lunch at the Hilltop Restaurant today with the mayor," said Andrea, while she removed the lids from the salads. "Guess the diner wasn't fancy enough for them. The mayor always takes people to the Hilltop when he's trying to impress them. Any other day of the week, he's eating at my place."

Macy, along with Missy Macintire, Rosie's granddaughter, arrived next. "Yay, food!" Macy cheered with a laugh, clapping her hands together. "I haven't eaten since breakfast. We were unbelievably busy all day today. I think every kid in the elementary school has the bug that's going around because they were all in our office today."

"Well, I have a date this weekend," said Missy, holding her hand to cover her mouth. "You better keep those germs to yourself." Missy walked over to give Rosie a hug, "Hi, Grandma. How was your day?"

"We had a good day here, Missy," hugging her back.

MaryAnn's ears perked up when her daughter said she had a date this weekend. "Anyone we know?" she asked, hopefully.

"Just a guy I met at college who's in town visiting relatives," Missy explained, winking at her grandmother. "His uncle is a chef at the Hilltop, and he invited me to have dinner with him there. It's nothing serious." She turned to give her own mother a hug. "No matchmaking, mom."

Missy knew her mother couldn't wait for her to settle down now that she had graduated from college. With her degree in business management, Missy hoped Hillary would soon change her status from full-time employee to manager of Everything's New Again Boutique, or possibly even business partner. She knew she could get a job in the city that easily paid double, but she loved her small town and didn't want to move. She also knew the number of eligible bachelors in Hope Springs was low.

"Oh, a mother can dream," sighed MaryAnn. And with that, everyone had a chuckle and got down to the business of eating.

"Has anyone seen Myrtle yet today?" asked Rosie, between bites.

"She came into the mercantile this morning complaining about all the strangers in town and wanting to know 'just what the dickens is going on?'" said Fran, using air quotes. "She said she and Candy would be here tonight, though."

Myrtle Freeman was one of Rosie's closest friends. She was one of those rare finds, also born and raised in Hope Springs. She and her late husband raised six children in their three-bedroom house. As understated as Rosie was, Myrtle was every bit and more as flamboyant. She loved her chunky necklaces and clip-on earrings. She had a cackle for a laugh, but almost always covered her mouth with her hand when she laughed, because she couldn't remember if she put her dentures in that morning.

Myrtle had worked hard all her life while raising her family. She and her husband were able to provide for their six children on a mill worker's salary; however, occasionally you might have seen her working behind the bar at the local establishment just outside of town, to make ends meet. She was also musically talented, playing anything from the organ and piano to the drums and banjo, all by ear. And when it came to her family and her beloved town, Myrtle was very protective. While five of her children had moved out of Hope Springs, her son Ben and daughter-in-law Candy, had stayed, raising their daughter, Luann, in Hope Springs.

"Does anyone know what the dickens is going on in this town?" shouted Myrtle as she came bounding through the door, Candy following behind and catching the door so it didn't slam. "We had to park three blocks down the street, and there are strangers everywhere." Myrtle declared as her chunky heels pounded across the hardwood floor.

"It seems that the town council is courting developers for their new revitalization project," Hillary informed her.

"Just what kind of revitalization are they talking about?" asked Myrtle, adjusting her flowery top down over her double-knit polyester pants. "I hope they aren't going to just tear stuff down and build new in its place. There is too much history in these old buildings to discard them like that."

"Now, Myrtle," Rosie admonished, "you and I have been around a long time and we've seen many changes in this place. Surely the town council will preserve the history of our beautiful town."

Myrtle just huffed and said she wasn't so sure since they were allowed to put in that chain drug store. She thought maybe the town council was a little too fond of change. "I don't know why everything has to be shiny and new," she lamented, shaking her head while her curly, home-dyed, red hair bounced back and forth.

This got all the women thinking since their businesses were all located on Main Street in the older buildings. Surely the town council would have to inform them if they were thinking about demolishing their buildings.

"Well, we all need to be vigilant, and if we hear something suspicious, let the others in the group know," suggested Myrtle. "Also, if the town council knows we are keeping an eye on them, they're less likely to make a move without the approval of the residents."

Chandler spoke up, "Actually, any changes in the town need to be brought before the residents in a public hearing before moving forward. It's in the town covenants."

"Well, if anyone should know, it's you, Chandler," Myrtle said. "We all think of you as the unofficial town historian, you know."

"I don't know about that," Chandler answered. "I just like knowing the history of our town and want to keep it as authentic as possible."

"Well, ladies, there isn't anything we can do about it now," said Rosie, "so let's just finish our dinner and get to work on our quilt. We have to have it done in three weeks for the United Methodist Women's Bazaar, and the stitches won't stitch themselves."

The current quilt-in-progress was a queen-size, double wedding ring quilt done in rose and green. The background fabric was a soft cream color. While the rings themselves were quilted along the pieced edge, or "stitched in the ditch", the cream areas between the locking rings were quilted with a beautiful feathering design. MaryAnn's job was to draw the feather design for everyone to stitch. Then Rosie taught each new quilter the art of hand quilting, and making sure each stitch was the same as the one before.

Money raised from this particular quilt would benefit local children in the area who were in need of new clothes for school.

"We've really come a long way on this in a short amount of time," said MaryAnn, as she sat down to stitch. "We're well over halfway done, so we should be able to finish in plenty of time for the bazaar."

"Rosie, you and Myrtle did a spectacular job of piecing this quilt," Fran complimented them. "I'm so impressed how each curve and seam intersection is perfectly matched."

"Thank you," said Rosie. "As much as I love the art of hand quilting, I do embrace wholeheartedly the art of machine piecing. It makes it go so much faster. Pinning the points at the intersections before you sew is a real lifesaver. And as I always say, press, press, press the seams before moving on to the next step."

"Of course, it doesn't hurt that we have done this particular pattern so many times we can do it in our sleep," Myrtle added.

Everyone settled into their respective chairs to continue their work from the week before. Myrtle steered the conversation toward the group's young, single baker.

"Chandler, how is your love life coming along?" she asked. Myrtle was nothing if not direct. She had known Chandler's late parents very well and felt like it was her duty to make sure their daughter found love in her life. Myrtle knew there had been a few guys throughout Chandler's college years, but none were able to meet her expectations. There had been a certain art gallery owner they had all thought was promising, but no one was really sure what had happened to bust up the romance.

"Non-existent," said Chandler, completing a row of stitching. "Of course, Sweet Stuff Bakery keeps me pretty busy, so I'm not really feeling like I need a man in my life." She was also glad it paid enough to support herself.

"We all need someone in our life," said Myrtle. She pulled her reading glasses off her face, letting them hang from their chain. "I've missed my late husband, Bill, for the past twenty-three years. It's still hard to believe he isn't going to come walking through the door."

"I don't know about that. My husband has been gone for over thirty years, and I haven't missed him at all," smiled Fran as she worked to thread her needle.

"But you got divorced," Myrtle said, shaking her arthritic finger at her. "That doesn't count."

"All I'm saying is, you don't need a man to have a fulfilling life. I've managed just fine on my own. Besides, if it weren't for the divorce settlement, I never would have been able to purchase the mercantile," said Fran, happy she finally got her needle threaded.

Macy had been listening intently to their conversation while trying to get her stitches to look like everyone else's. "But don't you sometimes wish you had someone to come home to every night?"

"Heavens no!" exclaimed Fran. "Then I'd have to do more work taking care of him."

"But maybe he would take care of you, instead," Macy said innocently.

"If you can find a man who would have your dinner ready when you get home instead of sitting on the couch waiting for you to cook for him, then you better hang on to him," said Fran, beginning to work on the feather pattern in front of her.

"Times have changed," said Myrtle. "More and more men are sharing in the household chores than when we were younger."

"All I can say is that I'm happy with my life just the way it is," answered Fran, defiantly.

"As ornery as you are, I doubt any man would have you anyway," exclaimed Myrtle. Everyone laughed at that, and Fran gave her a look meant to say she really didn't agree with that statement.

Chapter 5

Chandler listened to their conversation and wasn't sure what to think. She would love to have someone to share her day with when she came home. However, she wasn't sure she could put in a full day at the bakery and then have to come home and take care of someone else every night. Many nights she crashed on the couch with a bowl of cereal for dinner. She doubted any man would be okay with that.

Chandler had lived her entire life in Hope Springs, Virginia. Aside from going to college, she hadn't been out of the town much. She loved it there. Chandler's grandparents moved there from the country when her grandfather got a job at the Cotton Mill. They purchased a small two-bedroom, one-bath cottage within walking distance of the mill. The town center was just a two-block walk in the other direction.

Her parents had been high school sweethearts. Her father started working alongside his father at the Cotton Mill after graduation, and her parents were married later that summer. They rented one of the cottages across the street from the mill, and that was where Chandler spent the early part of her childhood.

Chandler still remembered that terrible rainy night her grandmother got the call about the accident. She was seven years old and staying with her grandparents while her parents took a trip to the city. On their way back, they were hit head-on by a drunk driver. There were no survivors.

Her grandparents raised her from that day on. Two years later, her grandfather passed away from a heart attack. Then it was up to Chandler and her grandmother to make a life for themselves. They were able to live off the money from her father and grandfather's life insurance and pensions. Luckily, there was also enough for her to go to college, debt free.

Chandler had always wanted to open her own bakery. Hope Springs didn't have one, and she knew she could make it a success. She learned everything she could from her grandmother about baking. They spent the majority of her childhood in the kitchen perfecting recipes for various cookies, pastries, pies, and cakes, until she went to college and earned a business degree. Her aging grandmother lived just long enough to see her open Sweet Stuff Bakery, passing away about a month after the grand opening.

That was over six years ago, Chandler thought with a small shake of her head. She began attending the weekly Advice Quilting Bee about four years earlier, and ever since then, Myrtle had been trying to marry her off. Chandler felt like she was some kind of special project for her.

"Well, Myrtle, so far I haven't found my Prince Charming, and I don't expect him to walk through that door any time soon," she said, pointing to the front door of the shop.

And wouldn't you know it, just then the door opened, and in walked someone who looked vaguely familiar to her.

"Who's that?" Macy loudly whispered as she looked toward the door, wide-eyed.

Everyone turned to see just who it was Macy was staring at.

"Oh, my goodness," exclaimed Rosie, getting up excitedly. "Peter, is that you?" She rushed toward the man she referred to as Peter standing just inside the front door.

"Grandmother Rosie!" Peter shouted, extending his arms to give her a hug.

"Who is Peter?" whispered Macy, still looking wide-eyed.

By now, almost everyone had dropped what they were doing to listen in. Everyone, that is, except Chandler. She knew exactly who he was, and she just couldn't believe he was here, standing in Rosie's shop. *"Grandmother Rosie?"* she repeated in her mind. Last time she had seen him was about ten months earlier that horrible night in the city after her breakup.

MaryAnn also knew who Peter was, and couldn't believe that out of the blue he had just walked through the door. "Peter Frederick is Ramona's son," MaryAnn whispered, watching on in bewilderment.

"Who is Ramona?" Macy whispered back in question.

"Ramona is Rosie's late daughter, and Peter's mother. She passed away three years ago," explained MaryAnn. "She left Hope Springs right after high school graduation and never looked back. Nearly broke Rosie's heart. Thank goodness Robert and I settled here so she would still have family close by."

"How come no one knew about Peter?" asked Macy.

"Ramona, her husband James, and Peter came to our wedding, when Peter was about five years old. They spent a week here during that summer," said MaryAnn. "All Ramona kept saying was that it was so much better in the city, and she couldn't understand how anyone would want to live here."

"She had made a big life for herself in high society," MaryAnn continued. "I know that Rosie keeps in touch with Peter during the holidays, but this is the first time he has come back to Hope Springs. I wonder why?"

42

Sitting there looking at Peter, Chandler couldn't help but wonder what kind of man would know about his extended family and not come to see them every chance he got. That would have been like gold to her. What she wouldn't give to have more time with her own family.

Chandler took a moment to look at the man she had met in the city at the sports bar. He still looked the same with his short, professionally cut, brown hair and chocolate brown eyes. Now, she could tell he was tall, probably over six feet. The way his custom suit fit, she figured he definitely had a gym membership. Everything about him oozed money and class.

"Oh, Peter, what brings you to Hope Springs?" asked Rosie excitedly, still holding on to him like she couldn't believe he was real.

"I was in the area on business, so I thought I'd stop by to see if I could take you to dinner," Peter explained with a bright smile.

"Well, you've come during our weekly Advice Quilting Bee, and I've already had my dinner," Rosie said, somewhat sadly. "But come on back and let me introduce you to my friends." She pulled him by the hand back to the quilting frame. "Peter, I'd like you to meet the ladies who keep me young," said Rosie, waiving her hand over the group. "This is Hillary Smith, owner of Everything's New Again Boutique. Next to her is Fran Mayfield, and she owns Hope Springs Mercantile. Of course, you remember Aunt MaryAnn and your cousin, Missy."

"Hello, Aunt MaryAnn. How is Uncle Robert doing?" asked Peter, walking over to her.

"He's as ornery as ever, but doing well," MaryAnn answered, getting up to give Peter a hug.

"And, Missy, I bet you're happy to be out of college," Peter said, giving Missy a hug as well.

"I am," she said, smiling. "I hope to be able to use my degree in business management here in Hope Springs."

"Well, if you have trouble finding something, please let me know. I know a few people," Peter said with a wink.

"Thanks," she said with a wider smile, sitting back down in her chair.

"Andrea Porter owns the Hope Springs Diner next door. She makes the best food in town," said Rosie proudly.

"Well, I look forward to trying it soon," Peter smiled at her.

"Anytime," Andrea answered, smiling proudly.

Rosie stood beside Myrtle next. "This is Myrtle, one of my closest friends."

"So nice to meet you, Myrtle," said Peter extending his hand.

"What's that hand for?" asked Myrtle. "If you're Rosie's grandson, then you're practically family," reaching out to give him a big hug. "And this is my daughter-in-law, Candy," she said pointing to Candy.

"How do you do, Peter?" asked Candy.

"So nice to meet you," said Peter absently. He had already moved on to the beautiful woman with auburn hair and deep green eyes. She looked familiar, but for the life of him he couldn't remember why.

"And who are you?" he asked, reaching out to shake her hand.

"This is Chandler Bradford," said Rosie. "She is the owner of Sweet Stuff Bakery."

"So nice to meet you," he said, with a wide smile.

"Hello," said Chandler, reaching out to shake his hand. It was then that she realized he didn't remember their previous meeting in the sports bar. *He really is full of himself,* she thought. The temptation to roll her eyes was strong, but she didn't want to insult Rosie. "And this is my friend, Macy," she said, trying to turn his attention in a different direction.

"Hi," said Macy, dreamily.

"Hi, Macy," he said shaking her hand, all the while looking at Chandler.

Macy gave up. She knew where his focus was. She sat back down and continued stitching.

"So, Chandler, what are you working on?" asked Peter, looking at the quilt on the frame.

"Rosie, why don't you explain to your grandson what this quilt is all about," Chandler said.

Peter tried to focus on what Rosie was saying, but in his mind he kept trying to figure out where he had seen the baker before. Rosie went on to explain who was going to benefit from this current project, but Peter only heard about half of what his grandmother was saying. He couldn't keep his eyes from going to Chandler. Never had anyone worked so hard at trying to ignore him. Just what was her story?

Who does this guy think he is? thought Chandler. She wished he would just stop staring at her and focus on his grandmother. It was clear that Rosie was so excited to see him. Chandler thought

45

she'd see if she could distract him. "What type of business brings you to Hope Springs?" Chandler asked. Did his business have something to do with the developers in town?

"Well, for the business question, there is some development potential outside of town. And as for what brings me here, my Grandmother Rosie, of course," he said, smiling. *Oh brother*, thought Chandler.

"Really?" Hillary's ears perked up. "What kind of development?"

"I'm sure you've seen the new construction going on out by the highway," he said. Seeing the ladies shake their heads in the affirmative, he continued. "My company is looking at other potential ventures as well."

What other potential ventures? thought Chandler. She wondered if he was with all the others courting the town council. "Well, we really love our small town, and we would hate for someone to change it."

"Sometimes change is good," Peter said, with a shrug of his shoulder and a charming smile. Usually Peter's smile could win over a crowd. But this was a tough one.

"Guess it depends on what kind of change you're talking about," said Myrtle gruffly. "I've seen where just a little bit of development can ruin the entire feel of a small town," she finished with her arms crossed.

"Yes," Fran agreed. "Look what happened to Forest Falls. Developers came in, tore down all the historic buildings, and put up contemporary new ones. It completely changed the town forever. It would have been nice if they could have just rehabilitated and renovated the historic ones. I've seen where that is all the rage on those home renovation shows now. They breathe new life into the old buildings instead of tearing them down."

"Some developers only see dollar signs," Myrtle said, with a pointed glance directed at Peter. "They only care how much money they will make, and not the historic value and character of the town."

Chandler could see Peter's demeanor change while listening to Fran and Myrtle's conversation. She wondered if maybe her hunch was right and he really was one of those developers lurking around town.

As if echoing her thoughts, Rosie looked up at Peter with a glance. "Surely you aren't one of those developers. Right, Peter?"

Good for you, thought Chandler, *be blunt*. He wouldn't be so heartless as to lie to his grandmother.

Peter turned to Rosie, smiled and said, "No, Grandmother, I'm not."

There was just something about Peter's demeanor that Chandler didn't trust. She couldn't put her finger on it, but she was sure that if she spent enough time around him, she'd be able to figure it out. But for Rosie's sake, Chandler hoped Peter was telling the truth, and was not part of the group that was looking to revitalize the town.

"How long are you in town?" asked MaryAnn, changing the subject. "Uncle Robert and I would love it if you could come over for dinner one night."

"I have to go back to the city tonight," said Peter. "However, I'm planning on making more trips in the future. I would love to see you then, Aunt MaryAnn."

"Where do you stay when you come to town?" asked Macy.

"Even though it's only about an hour's drive to the city," Peter explained, "When we're here on business for more than a day, my team and I stay in one of the hotels outside of town."

About three years earlier, a few of the farmers sold their properties near the highway to a development firm. Ever since, fast food restaurants, hotels, and a strip mall had popped up. Chandler knew that there was still more land to be developed in that area.

"Oh, I wish I had known you were coming," said Rosie. "You could have stayed with me!"

"Thank you for the offer, Grandmother. However, there are several of us from my office staying there. It makes more sense for me to stay with my team."

"Well, next time you come, maybe one of us could show you around town," offered Myrtle, looking straight at Chandler.

Chandler did her very best not to shoot daggers at Myrtle. "Well, I'm really busy with the bakery right now, Myrtle," she said, a bit sternly.

"Maybe your assistant could handle things for a few hours while you show Peter around? You do know more about the history of this town than anyone, Chandler," Myrtle replied, slyly.

Chandler wasn't sure how she was going to weasel out of this one with Peter's grandmother standing right there. Seriously, she could have strangled Myrtle right then and have no remorse.

Peter saved her from having to comment further. "I'd love to have you show me around the next time I'm in town, if it wouldn't be too much trouble. I haven't been back here since I was a little boy, and I'd love to get reacquainted. I think I may have time later next week, if you're free?"

"There you go," Myrtle said, sitting back in her chair with a wide smile on her face.

"I'll have to look at my schedule at the bakery and see if I have any available free time. Graduations are coming up and I'll be getting hit with cake orders and the like." Chandler was pretty pleased with herself on coming up with that excuse on the fly.

That's it! Thought Peter. *She was the baker in Crandy's!* Instead of admitting they had met before and causing the ladies to ask more questions, he simply said, "I'll call you later in the week and see if you have an opening in your schedule." He continued on by saying that he should be going, and hoped Rosie didn't mind if she started seeing more of him. Of course, Rosie was thrilled at the prospect. Chandler, not so much.

Peter said his goodbyes to the ladies and that he looked forward to seeing them all again soon.

"I'll walk you out," said Rosie.

After they left, Myrtle turned her attention to Chandler. "You know, Chandler, it wouldn't kill you to give the guy a tour. He seemed perfectly harmless to me."

"Yeah, Chandler, what gives?" Hillary asked. "Peter is definitely attracted to you."

"He barely noticed me when Rosie introduced us," said Macy dejectedly.

"He's really not my type," Chandler said. "And there's just something about him that doesn't feel right." Chandler also didn't want to let on that she had seen him in his natural habitat that terrible night in the city after the art gallery opening, and that he had completely forgotten about her. After her past, and the fact that he was obviously just another guy who viewed women as a dime a dozen, Chandler really didn't want to get involved with someone anytime soon, and especially not a man from the city who clearly didn't appreciate the small-town way of life.

Andrea was usually pretty quiet and didn't offer much to the conversation, but even she had to stop her stitching to speak up. "What part about him troubles you, the handsome looks or the fact that he clearly has a lucrative business?"

"Exactly," Fran agreed. "If a man like that had shown any interest in me, I would have remarried in a heartbeat."

Conversation ceased when Rosie came back to take her seat at the frame. "Wasn't it a wonderful surprise having Peter stop by? I'm so glad we'll be seeing more of him. And he seemed quite interested in you, Chandler."

Chandler just smiled and kept on stitching. She couldn't put her finger on it, but there was definitely something he wasn't telling them about why he was in Hope Springs.

Chapter 6

I'm a good judge of character, thought Peter as he drove back to the city. He had a great group of friends, and if he wanted he could easily have a different date every night of the week. What was it about Chandler Bradford? It wasn't like she was the prettiest girl he'd ever met. She was definitely not the most sophisticated. So why couldn't he get her out of his mind?

He thought back to their last meeting when he saw her in Crandy's. She had mentioned something about being at an art gallery before going there, so she must have some connections in the city. All he really remembered was the mention of the art gallery, she loved the Crusaders, and that she was a baker. Not much to go on.

He recalled watching her walk in at Crandy's, but he couldn't remember if her height was due to high heeled shoes she was wearing or not. This time, she had her hair pulled back in a ponytail, wore very little in the way of make-up, and was dressed in a Sweet Stuff Bakery t-shirt and jeans. Definitely more understated than the green dress she had worn the last time they'd met. Then there were her emerald green eyes. Peter could never forget those eyes. Against the backdrop of her auburn hair, they really were striking.

Her demeanor left a lot to be desired, however. He could tell she wasn't impressed with him. Usually women fell all over themselves trying to talk to him, but not this one. She seemed like she didn't want to have anything to do with him.

Why?

What was so wrong with him that she didn't want to give him the time of day, and why was he so worried about it? That thought was with him the rest of the drive home.

As Peter walked into the lobby of his condo, Chandler was still on his mind.

"Good evening, Mr. Frederick," Carl the doorman greeted him as he held the front door open for Peter. Peter loved the fact that his building came with doormen dressed in attire like you would see in an old Hollywood movie. It made the place seem classy.

"Good evening, Carl," Peter said with a smile. "How is your family doing?"

"All good," answered Carl. "Did you have a good trip to Hope Springs?" Peter always let the staff know when he was going to be away and where he would be.

"It was definitely interesting," Peter told him. "I saw my Grandmother Rosie for the first time in a long while."

"Oh, that's wonderful. I'm sure she was happy to see you," Carl replied. But sensing there was more, he added "my guess is that isn't what's got you preoccupied."

Peter always thought Carl was astute. "Well, I met this woman at my grandmother's store, and I just can't get her out of my mind," explained Peter.

"Oh, is she single?" asked Carl with a raised eyebrow.

"Yes, I believe she is."

"Is she pretty?"

"I suppose so in that small town girl sort of way."

"So, when are you gonna ask her out?" Peter knew that Carl was a happily married man with three teenage children. He was always interested in who Peter was dating. So far, none of the women Peter had brought through the door impressed Carl. And for some strange reason, Peter valued the doorman's opinion on the topic.

Peter smiled. "She owns the local bakery, and mentioned she is going to be busy with graduation cake orders. However, I may try to see her again next week." When Peter saw Carl get a big grin on his face, he held up one hand and went on to explain "Not for a date. She is giving me a town history tour."

Carl clapped his hands, "That works too! It's about time you went out with a girl who isn't from the city. Someone more down to earth is just what you need."

"You think so?" asked Peter, wondering how Carl knew just what he needed.

"Definitely," Carl said enthusiastically.

"I'll have to think about that," said Peter, absently. "Have a good evening, Carl," he added as he walked away.

"You too, Mr. Frederick," Carl replied, smiling.

As Peter continued on to the elevator that would take him to the fifteenth floor, he thought about Carl's last comment. *Do I really need someone who isn't from the city?* He thought. *Is that what's lacking in my life?*

He exited the elevator and walked to the door leading into his penthouse. Upon entering, he took a look around. The spacious foyer opened to a magnificent view of the city through a bank of floor to ceiling windows. Off to the right, the well-equipped kitchen overlooked the living and dining areas providing the consummate entertaining space, not that Peter did much entertaining. Everything about the condo was high end, and also very sterile and impersonal. He had no pictures of family or anything telling who he was. The master bedroom to the left also gave the same impression, and why he needed a television in the master bathroom was beyond him. He never used it, but it came with the place. *Guess that is what happens when you hand a high-priced decorator your credit card and say to take care of everything.*

This got him to wondering what type of home Chandler Bradford lived in. He was sure it probably looked nothing like this. But really, why did he care what Chandler's home looked like, and what she might think of his?

He walked into his office and looked around. This room was done in browns and tans, which gave a warmer feel than the rest of the house. *At least in here there is a color other than gray,* he thought, pulling his laptop out of his briefcase and placing it on his desk.

He sat down at his mahogany desk and turned on his laptop. As it was booting up, he decided to listen to the messages left on his cell phone.

The first was from his secretary, Pat, reminding him of a meeting he had the next day regarding a project that was wrapping up in the city.

The second was from his assistant, Cassia Collins.

"Where are you, Peter?" he heard Cassia say frantically. "I have been trying to reach you so we can discuss what we found in Hope Springs. Please call me ASAP!"

Ugh, he didn't want to deal with Cassia right now. He was tired and in no mood for her dramatics. He'd hired Cassia two years earlier, at the request of her father, who had just wanted her to get a job so he could stop supporting her. She had a business degree, but no real desire to work for a living. Richard Collins had called Peter and practically begged him to hire her. Since Richard had given Peter his start, he couldn't very well say no.

As it turned out, Cassia had surprised everyone with a natural knack for business, better than even she, herself, had expected. She was able to manage a couple of development projects in the city, seeing them through from start to finish. Unfortunately, one big flaw was her flair for the dramatic. He had her on his team going to Hope Springs on the scouting mission. Before they decided to do a project, a team from Frederick Development, Inc. went ahead to see if it was worth it. He wasn't sure he wanted to hear what Cassia had to say, after hearing the ladies talk at his grandmother's shop.

Peter looked at his watch and decided that anything Cassia had to say could wait until he got into the office in the morning. He quickly scanned his email inbox, and since there was nothing urgent, shut his computer down for the night. He'd get a good night's sleep and deal with everything in the morning.

Chapter 7

Chandler left Rosie's with a lot on her mind. She didn't like hearing that the town council was looking into development, and there were just too many questions surrounding this sudden influx of visitors. She was worried about her shop, and those of the other women.

But, mostly, she couldn't seem to get Peter Frederick out of her mind. Myrtle was really pushing for her to go out with him, but she wasn't sure she needed that right now. Plus, Peter really wasn't her type. He was definitely big city class, and she liked her men more salt of the earth. Jeans and a beer versus suits and a martini. He seemed a bit too sure of himself.

As she walked past Hope Springs Diner and on toward Everything's New Again Boutique, she couldn't help but think about her friends and their businesses. Everyone had worked so hard to build them. Sure, the actual structures needed work, but the businesses themselves were very successful. It was amazing to watch Hillary run the boutique and still be able to care for her two small children. She knew that having Missy work there full-time had helped a lot. The boutique shared building space with Hillary's husband Jack. His accounting firm handled all of the accounting business for the ladies of the group.

Chandler turned left at the corner and headed down Spring Street, past the Hope Springs Post Office to her right. She loved the fact that she could walk to almost everything she needed. Once a week she made the drive out to the large grocery store by the highway, but other than that the mercantile carried most everything she needed.

As she continued down Spring Street, she said hello to her neighbors. Chandler knew pretty much everyone in town; however, there were new families moving in all the time and fixing up the cottages around her. She enjoyed working on her own house as well.

It was on these nightly walks that Chandler could clear her head and relax her body. The neighborhood was peaceful and quiet, and there was no traffic noise to contend with. She wondered if Peter could live in a small town. The city was so vastly different and she wasn't sure he could handle a place like Hope Springs. Every time she had to go into the city for business for the bakery, she couldn't wait to get back home.

As Chandler came up to her house, she couldn't help but burst with pride. It wasn't a mansion like those on the other side of Main Street, but she didn't need anything that big. This was her family home, and she took great care in the upkeep. She adored the exterior mint green painted wood siding with its fuchsia front door. On a beautiful summer evening, she loved sitting on the wide front porch with a glass of wine and watching the world go by. And when she walked through the door, the home was warm and inviting, with walls and tongue and groove paneled ceiling both painted a warm cream color.

She went down the hall to the kitchen and poured herself a glass of wine to drink on the front porch. As she was pouring, she heard a knock at the front door. Peering around the corner, she saw that it was Macy.

Motioning for her to come in, she said, "Would you like a glass of wine?"

"Do you even have to ask?" Macy answered, smiling.

"Let's go sit on the front porch," Chandler said as she handed Macy a glass. She grabbed the bottle as well. It was a beautiful night, after all, and they might be there for a while. Besides, Macy lived across the street, so she didn't have far to walk.

Each of them took a seat and put their feet up on the ottoman. "This is so nice," said Macy, running her fingers through her hair. "I wish my landlord would let me do something with the front porch. Every time I ask, he says, 'sure, if you want to pay for it'! My goal is to buy one of these homes for myself so I can do with it what I want."

"I was very fortunate that I inherited it from my grandmother, God rest her soul," Chandler said. "I miss her every day, but at least I have the house and wonderful memories."

"So, what do you think about what happened at Rosie's?" asked Macy, taking a sip of her wine.

Chandler knew this was why she stopped by. "I think we got a lot done on the quilt."

"That's not what I'm talking about, and you know it," Macy admonished.

"I know," teased Chandler. "Honestly, I'm not sure what to think about Mr. Frederick."

"Well, I think he's a dream," Macy said. "But he's clearly interested in you," she added, tipping her glass toward Chandler.

"Oh, I don't know," Chandler answered. "I've seen enough guys like him to know they think all they have to do is smile at a woman and she's theirs. I'm not interested in being any man's small-town conquest." She'd had enough of that in college.

Macy agreed, "that was one of the things I hated when I tried to date before coming here. But maybe Peter's different."

"I don't know," Chandler hedged, taking a sip of her wine. "I'm not sure I want to pursue anything with Rosie's grandson. What if it doesn't work out? That could be very awkward, especially because of how close we all are." Chandler still wasn't sure she wanted the other ladies to know she had already seen Peter in his natural habitat.

Macy was one of the few people who knew about Chandler's relationship with Victor Confer, the owner of an art gallery in the city. He had hired Chandler to provide baked goods for his gallery openings, and eventually they started dating. Chandler learned Victor hadn't been completely honest with her about his personal life and had broken it off, and coincidently, that same night she had run into Peter in a sports bar in the city. Chandler couldn't tell for sure, but she was fairly certain by his reaction earlier, he hadn't remembered their first encounter.

"I can see where you're coming from," said Macy, "but maybe this time *will* be different. From what I remember you telling me, the last guy just used you for your baking skills. And you aren't going to find anyone here who even compares to Peter."

"Now, Macy, you haven't even lived here that long. Can you honestly tell me you've met every eligible bachelor in Hope Springs?"

"No, but *you've* lived here your whole life and still haven't found someone!" Macy countered.

"Good point," Chandler said with a laugh, taking a sip of her wine. "I'm going to have to think about this one. Maybe I'll invite MaryAnn over for coffee at the bakery and pick her brain."

"Speaking of the bakery, are you really that busy?" Macy asked, referring to the excuse Chandler had used earlier.

"Believe it or not, that wasn't a lie. We have a lot of graduation cakes to make this week, and Gretchen is my only assistant. Candy mentioned that her daughter, Luann, is home from college for the summer. I might give her a call to see if she's available to help out."

"Isn't she the one who wants to open a bed and breakfast in Hope Springs once she graduates?" asked Macy.

"That's right, she is," Chandler said, pointing her finger at Macy. "She might want to learn how to do some of the baking for that. I'll definitely give her a call tomorrow to see if she's interested."

Before they knew it, they had finished off the bottle of wine. "Guess it's time to call it a night," said Chandler, looking at the empty bottle.

"Did we really just drink the whole thing?" asked Macy, staring at the empty bottle. "Hope I can find my way home," she said, smiling.

"Guess we'll both sleep well tonight!"

Macy left, and Chandler went in the house thinking how nice it was to have her so close by. She had only lived in Hope Springs a year, but it felt like they had known each other all their lives. Chandler rinsed out the bottle for recycling, and put both wine glasses in the dishwasher.

With a plan in place to contact both MaryAnn and Luann in the morning, Chandler turned off the lights and went to bed.

Chapter 8

Chandler woke the next morning feeling refreshed and ready to tackle the day ahead. As she went through her morning routine, she made a mental note to call Candy when she got to the bakery. Her next call would be to MaryAnn to invite her to the bakery for pastries. It was time to find out all she could about Peter Frederick.

As she walked into the kitchen to turn on her coffee maker, Chandler heard a knock on the door. She glanced at the clock and realized she was moving slower than she thought. It was mornings like this Chandler was grateful for Gretchen. She would have already been hard at work preparing the morning's baked goods. It couldn't be Macy because she would be headed to the clinic.

Chandler turned to walk down the hall and saw Myrtle at her front door. *Ugh*, she thought, *it is way too early for this*. Especially, since she hadn't had her coffee yet.

"Good morning, Myrtle," Chandler said, opening the door and moving aside for her to enter.

"I sure hope it's going to be a good morning," said Myrtle as she walked past Chandler and into her small living/dining room. "Would you mind explaining to me why you don't want to go out with Peter Frederick? I promised your grandmother I would watch after you, and I've failed miserably up until now," she finished dejectedly slumping her shoulders.

"What do you mean, you promised, and how have you failed miserably?" Chandler asked suspiciously, knowing a guilt trip when she heard one.

"Are you married yet?" Myrtle asked.

"No."

"Are you even dating anyone?" she asked pointing her finger at Chandler.

Chandler was really getting tired of this line of questioning. "No," she answered, probably a little more forcefully than she should have with the older woman. She knew Myrtle only had the best of intentions for her.

"Then I've failed miserably," Myrtle said, slumping her shoulders again.

Chandler took a minute to look at Myrtle. Today, her attire was lime green spandex pants, bright pink sneakers, an oversized white t-shirt with a giant, orange flower on the front, and a headband corralling her bright red hair. She looked like she just walked off the set of one of those old exercise videos popular in the 1980s. "Where have you been already this morning?""I've been to the church exercise class," Myrtle explained. "Every Friday morning, we meet at 7:00 to exercise to a 1980s exercise video."

"That explains it," Chandler said dryly.

"Stop trying to dodge the question, young lady," Myrtle scolded. "What's wrong with Peter Frederick?"

"I thought I explained myself very clearly last night," Chandler said, walking down the hall to the kitchen.

Myrtle was hot on her heels, "Oh, that's right. You're too busy at the bakery, and you have a 'feeling'," she said using air quotes. "Well then, I think it's about time you got yourself some more help at the bakery. Gretchen is a great assistant baker, but you need someone to help you with the customers."

"You're right," Chandler said, remembering her conversation with Macy. She knew that Myrtle loved feeling that she was coming up with a new idea, so she asked, "Do you know of anyone looking for summer employment?"

"I bet Luann would be interested!" Myrtle practically shouted. "She just got home from college for the summer, and she would be great at the shop!"

"Okay, can you give me her number and I'll call her to see if she can come in this morning?" Myrtle gave her Luann's cell phone number. Chandler hoped that would be enough to satisfy her for the day, but unfortunately Myrtle's mind was too sharp.

"So, now that we got that taken care of, answer my question about Peter." Myrtle crossed her arms over her flowered shirt and leaned again the counter, signaling she wasn't going anywhere until she got answers for the real reason she'd come over.

Chandler took her time putting the coffee pod in the machine, pushing the start button on the biggest serving size, and waiting for it to brew before she answered. She really needed caffeine in the morning to deal with Myrtle, especially dressed like that.

After she took a sip she said, "I'm just not sure I want to start something with Rosie's grandson. What if it doesn't work out? That could get really awkward, don't you think?"

Myrtle shook her head from side to side. "How do you know it won't work out?"

"Myrtle, he and I are nothing alike," Chandler stated, trying to explain her reasons for not wanting to start something with Peter Frederick. "I hate the big city life, and he oozes it. I can't picture him giving that up to live in Hope Springs."

"I realize the last guy from the city didn't work out, but that doesn't mean this one won't either," Myrtle interjected. "Besides, I'm not asking you to marry him tomorrow," she said, forcefully.

"Plus, I have a feeling he is not being completely honest about why he was here in the first place," Chandler countered.

"Look," Myrtle said waiving her hand, "just give him a tour of our town. And if you have this feeling that he's up to no good, you can show him exactly what our town has to offer and why it needs to stay small."

Chandler paused for a moment. Myrtle did have a point there. "Alright, I'll give it some more thought," she conceded, trying to appease Myrtle.

Looking at her clock over the kitchen sink, Chandler said, "I'm already late for work and I haven't even showered yet." As she moved Myrtle toward the front door, she added, "Thanks so much for giving me Luann's number. I'll call her when I get to the shop."

"Keep me posted, dear," Myrtle said hugging her. "You know I only have your best interests at heart."

"I know. I'll keep you posted." Chandler closed the door and then raced around trying to get ready for work. At least Myrtle had taken care of the phone call to Candy. She'd do the rest once she got to the bakery.

Chapter 9

Peter Frederick was never a morning person, but he got up anyway and headed for the gym. He always met his college roommate, Jake Grainger, there to work out before they both set off to work. Jake, or Dr. Grainger as he was now called, was finishing up his residency at City Hospital. Once he was finished, he wanted to go into private practice.

"Good morning," Jake said as they both began their workout.

"Morning," mumbled Peter, still trying to get motivated to work out.

"Rough night last night?" asked Jake, having seen Peter in this state many a morning after a night on the town with one of his many lady friends.

"It's not what you think," Peter replied. "I got back late from Hope Springs, and had a hard time falling asleep." Peter had spent most of his night tossing and turning. He just couldn't get those emerald green eyes out of his mind. Every time he closed his eyes, those eyes were staring back at him.

"Oh, that's right. I forgot you went down there on business," Jake said. "Didn't you say you have family there as well?"

"Yes, my grandmother owns a quilting shop in town, so I stopped in to see her. For someone who is eighty-three, you'd never know it. She has more energy than someone half her age. She said the ladies of the Advice Quilting Bee keep her young," Peter said, moving to the next machine.

Jake took over the machine Peter just vacated. "The what?"

Peter explained the Advice Quilting Bee and their function. "It's really kind of cool. They all put their skills toward a common goal and get a lot accomplished for a good cause."

"And that's what kept you up all night? Ladies quilting?" asked Jake, incredulously.

"No, not all of them. Just one," Peter said, taking a drink of water.

"Oh, now we're getting somewhere," Jake said with an emphasis on the 'Oh', "What's her name?"

"Her name is Chandler Bradford, and she owns Sweet Stuff Bakery in Hope Springs. It's not that she's any prettier than anyone else I've gone out with," Peter explained, "but I've never seen eyes so emerald green before. I just kept seeing those eyes every time I tried to fall asleep."
"So, knowing you, you asked her out, right?" Jake hedged, smiling.

Peter moved on to the next machine without answering. He loaded more weight on than he probably should have, and took his frustration out on the machine. This didn't go unnoticed by Jake.

"Ah hah! She turned you down, didn't she?" Jake knew that, in the city, most women jumped at the chance to go out with Peter Frederick. He couldn't remember the last time a woman rejected him.

Peter stopped the machine and looked at his friend. "Yes," he said while trying to catch his breath. "She said she was too busy at the bakery to go out with me," he added, like it was the most absurd thing anyone had ever told him. Peter couldn't remember the last time a woman had turned him down!

"Uh huh," said Jake smiling.

"What's that smile for?" Peter asked.

"You really like this girl, don't you?" Jake asked, looking directly at Peter.

"I don't know," Peter answered, frustratingly running his fingers through his hair. "She wouldn't even get up out of her chair to shake my hand. For all I know she may only be three feet tall!"

"Do you really believe that?" Jake asked, with a wry smile.
"No, I don't." Peter went on to explain her long, auburn hair in the ponytail, clean complexion void of makeup, and no nonsense jeans and t-shirt. "She's not my type at all. That's what's so frustrating."

"So, what are you going to do about it?" asked Jake, finishing up the last of his workout.

"I don't know," said Peter. He finished his workout and they both headed out to get showers and head to work.

Peter wasn't sure he was ready to face whatever drama was going to hit him at the office. Maybe they should just cross Hope Springs off the potential development list.

Peter got to the office around 7:45 a.m. and looked at his desk. It was full of notes, contracts, and other important papers he should probably be dealing with. Unfortunately, he couldn't concentrate on any of them.

He took out his cell phone and looked up Sweet Stuff Bakery, Hope Springs, Virginia, on the internet. He tapped on the link to call the shop and waited. *Damn*, he thought, *the answering machine.*

"Hi, this is Chandler from Sweet Stuff Bakery. We are elbow deep in dough right now and can't come to the phone. Please leave a message and we'll call you back as soon as we get these sweet treats into the oven."

Peter waited for the beep. "Hi, this is Peter Frederick. I met you last night at my grandmother's quilting shop. I was wondering if you would have time next week to show me around the town. I believe Myrtle mentioned you know a lot about the history of the town, and I'm very interested in learning about it. Please call me when your hands are not elbow deep in dough, at 555-843-2954. I look forward to talking to you soon." *There*, he thought, *now the ball is in her court.*

Chapter 10

Chandler walked into the bakery to the smell of baking bread and cinnamon. Gretchen had already been hard at work baking cinnamon rolls, pastries, and bread to fill the cases for the morning rush. She had also already started the coffee to be sold with the morning fare. Chandler made a mental note to give her a raise as soon as her finances would allow.

"Good morning, Gretchen," Chandler said. "You've already been busy, I see." Chandler really didn't know what she would do without Gretchen. It was just past 8:00 in the morning and Gretchen already had everything ready for their 9:00 a.m. open time. Next up would be cookies and cakes.

"Howdy," said Gretchen working on the chocolate chip cookies. "Take a listen to the answering machine. The phone has already been ringing, but I let it go to the machine since we aren't open yet."

Chandler got a pad of paper and pen ready to write down messages and hit the button. The first was from a mom wanting to order a cake for her son's graduation party. Chandler wrote down the number so she could call her back. The second was from a girl wanting to order a wedding shower cake. She did the same as the first and would call her back later. The third really piqued her interest. It was a call from Peter Frederick.

Chandler listened to his message.

"Who is Peter Frederick?" asked Gretchen, sliding the last of three trays of unbaked chocolate chip cookies across the counter.

"Rosie Macintire's grandson. I met him last night at her shop. He was here on business," Chandler answered. She placed the cookie dough-loaded trays in the oven.

"What kind of business would bring him to Hope Springs?" Gretchen asked as she moved on to the peanut butter cookies. Some bakeries liked to produce gourmet flavored cookies, but Chandler and Gretchen found that their best sellers were regular chocolate chip, peanut butter, oatmeal raisin, and sugar cookies decorated with sprinkles. If a holiday was coming up, the sugar cookies would be decorated accordingly.

"Good question," Chandler answered. "We all just hope he isn't one of those developers who have been hanging around the past couple of weeks."

Gretchen continued working on the cookies. "I went to the Hilltop for dinner last night with my husband, and I overheard the mayor sounding all high and mighty to some folks I didn't recognize, saying that the entire town is very excited about the revitalization project."

"Well, since we don't really know what this project is, how can we be excited about it?" Chandler asked, skeptically. "Anyway, I need to make a couple of calls before I call him back and before we open. I was going to give Luann a call to see if she wanted to work with us this summer. We really could use the help."

"That sounds like a great idea," said Gretchen, excitedly. "We have more and more orders for cakes coming in every day, and we could use help with the regular stuff."

As Chandler dialed Luann's number, her mind went back to the message left by Peter and her earlier conversation with Myrtle.

70

Maybe the best way to see what he was up to was to meet with him and give him a tour. She still wanted to talk to MaryAnn first.

"Hello," Luann answered quizzically, not recognizing the number on caller i.d.

"Hi Luann, it's Chandler Bradford at Sweet Stuff," Chandler explained.

"Oh, hi!" Luann said excitedly. "I didn't recognize the number, but my grandma said you'd be calling."

Of course, she did, thought Chandler. *Only Myrtle would call ahead to give Luann the heads up.* "Then I guess you already know why I'm calling," she said.

"Yes, and I'd love to come in for an interview," Luann answered. "I'm free anytime."

Chandler looked at the daily schedule hanging over the desk. "How does 3:00 this afternoon work?"

"Works fine," Luann told her.

"Great! See you then," Chandler said before hanging up the phone.

Chandler's next call was to MaryAnn. She wanted to find out all MaryAnn knew about her nephew before she called him.

MaryAnn said she'd be over around 10:00 a.m., after the morning bakery crowd died down. "But save me a cinnamon roll and some coffee," she told her. "I know how fast your morning baked goods sell out."

"Will do," said Chandler. "See you around ten."

The call to Peter could wait until after she got her work done and talked to MaryAnn. It was now 8:45 a.m. and they opened at 9:00 a.m. She got the cash register all squared way, checked the coffee, and made sure everything was ready in the display cases. The first hour was always the busiest, and then she could take a break. She'd also call the two cake orders after her visit from MaryAnn. Her shop was busy, but she wouldn't have it any other way.

Chapter 11

"Peter Frederick, why didn't you return my call last night?" Cassia Collins shouted as she bounded into Peter's office past Pat, his secretary.

Pat gave Peter a look that said, 'I'm sorry,' and then shut the door. Normally, she would offer his visitor coffee, he thought wryly. He knew Pat's opinion of Cassia was less than positive, despite her business success.

"I got in late last night and was too tired to talk to anyone," he answered, not understanding why he needed to defend himself.

"Well, I'm not just anyone and you know it," she said suggestively. Peter noticed her skirt was particularly short and tight, and pushing the boundaries of proper office attire. He found himself wondering how Chandler would look in the same outfit, and then realized he shouldn't be thinking about that.

"Your voicemail said you wanted to discuss the project," he said, ignoring her suggestion. "What's up?"

"Mayor Thompson is such a pushover; this is going to be a piece of cake. He's all for tearing down the old, decrepit buildings and putting up brand new, contemporary ones in their place," Cassia said looking down at her perfectly manicured fingernails. Peter once again found himself thinking about Chandler. He couldn't remember if her nails were painted, but he'd bet money they weren't.

"What about all the history in the buildings?" Peter asked. "Doesn't he care about that?" From what he'd heard the previous night, the mayor may be in the minority on that sentiment.

"He didn't seem to," Cassia said, shrugging her shoulders. "Once I told him about the business and tax revenue we could be bringing into the town, all he saw were dollar signs."

"Alright, let me see the plan you have and which buildings we're looking at."

Cassia rolled out the blueprint containing the plans for a revitalized Hope Springs. Pretty much any building that was historical by more than one hundred years was being torn down. Peter was happy, however, to see that his grandmother's building was not included in the demolition. From what he had seen the previous night, it was in good shape.

"See, your grandmother's shop would stay, as would the Hope Springs Diner. The next two blocks would be razed. This includes a consignment shop, the post office and visitor center on one side, and the bakery and library across the street," Cassia said. "My assistant took pictures of the buildings to be torn down," she said, handing Peter a stack of photos. "As you can see, they are in sad shape. I honestly don't know how some of them are still standing. The consignment shop looks like it's been redone, but the mayor is okay with it going so that we have the room for the office buildings he wants."

Peter took the stack of photos. *Damn,* he thought. He had hoped the bakery would not be on the chopping block, and he was sure they would get pushback from the community about the library. He quickly looked through the photos and decided he should check out each building in person, on his next visit to town.

He was beginning to think he should have gone to dinner with Cassia when she met with the mayor, instead of visiting his grandmother.

"When is our next meeting with the mayor?" Peter asked, handing the stack back to Cassia. He wanted to meet with Chandler first since she seemed to be the local historian. He was usually the first to give the go ahead for demolition when the buildings were just too dilapidated to save, but he had a feeling there was a good bit of history involved with these structures, and he wanted to make sure before they announced their plans.

"Not for a few weeks," Cassia replied, rolling up the plans and gathering up all the photos. She placed the photos in her briefcase and closed it tight. "The mayor wanted to work on the town council first."

"Let's try to keep this one close to the vest for a while. Something tells me that not everyone in the town will be on board," Peter said, picking up the rolled plans and ushering Cassia toward the door.

Cassia turned toward Peter when they reached the door. "How about taking me to lunch today?" she asked suggestively.

"Oh, I'm going to be spending a lot of today catching up on what happened around here while I was out," Peter answered as he opened the door for Cassia to walk out.

Cassia pouted her lips. "You have to eat lunch, sometime."

"I'll have Pat order something in," was his answer, handing her the plans. He knew Cassia was always trying to make their relationship more than professional, and he just wasn't interested.

"Alright," Cassia said dejectedly. "I'll call the mayor and tell him to get working on the town council."

As he watched Cassia walk out in a huff, he noticed Pat had a slight grin on her usually serious face. Pat had been Peter's secretary since his company began. She was a married mother of two teenage boys, and sometimes treated Peter like he was one of them. He kind of liked the fact that she took care of him now and then. "Pat, can you order something for me for lunch, so the excuse you just heard is legit?"

"Sure thing, Mexican or Italian?" Pat asked pulling up her stack of menus from a drawer file.

"Surprise me," Peter answered as he walked back into his office.

As he gazed out the expansive office window on the thirtieth floor, the view of the city was breathtaking. Peter's office high-rise overlooked the river that cut the city in half. This side was the newer, more developed half. Across the river, the buildings were much older, with some predating the Civil War. He thought about all the historical buildings there. He was sure that if a developer came and wanted to raze them there would be a huge uproar.

He then pictured what would happen if he proposed the same for Hope Springs. From what he'd heard the previous evening, he could see Myrtle in her bright outfit, holding a sign, leading the others down Main Street, and standing in front of his construction equipment. That thought made him smile.

Peter turned his back to the view and looked at the chaos on his desk. He decided he couldn't stand here all day waiting for Chandler to get back to him. He'd better get busy and get some work done.

Chapter 12

True to her word, MaryAnn came through the door of the bakery right at 10:00 a.m. "Sure hope you have my coffee and cinnamon roll ready," she announced. "I'm starving and ready for a sugar break."

"Right here," Chandler said as she walked toward one of the small tables set up in front by the window. "The roll is warm and the coffee is piping hot. Have a seat."

MaryAnn took a bite of roll and a sip of coffee. "Yum, you definitely make the best in town." MaryAnn took another bite and sip of her coffee. "So, I'm guessing you want the lowdown on my nephew."

Chandler smiled. "How did you know I wanted to talk to you about Peter?"

MaryAnn looked up at her over her coffee cup with a look that said, 'Do you really have to ask?'

"Myrtle," Chandler said matter-of-factly. She had learned a long time ago there were no secrets in a small town.

"So what do you want to know?" MaryAnn asked, sitting back in her chair.

"What is he really like?" Chandler asked. "I was having a hard time last night deciding if he was genuinely that nice, or if that was a front for Rosie."

"Well, from what I know of him, he is really that nice. I haven't gotten to spend too much time with him, but he did build his business from the ground up, and works really hard at it," MaryAnn said, taking another bite of her roll.

"Why hasn't he come to visit Rosie more often?" Chandler inquired, getting up to get MaryAnn a coffee refill. "If I still had family living, and I was this close, I'd be visiting them as often as I could."

"I know his mother hated living in Hope Springs, and that's why she only brought him here once as a child," MaryAnn remarked, taking her refilled cup from Chandler's outstretched hands. "Maybe she somehow influenced his decision not to visit here as an adult. But regardless, Rosie was thrilled to see him, and he seemed quite interested in you," MaryAnn said with a pointed look as she finished the last of her cinnamon roll.

"Do you think he has anything to do with this revitalization plan?" Chandler asked, ignoring the last comment.

"I asked Robert about that this morning," MaryAnn said. "He wasn't sure, but didn't think he would be. He said there was some woman who has been courting the mayor, so he figured it was her company."

"Myrtle says that if I think he is behind it, then all the more reason for me to give him the grand tour and sell him on all the history," Chandler said, taking a sip of her own coffee.

"I think you're a good judge of character," MaryAnn agreed, "and would know pretty quickly what his intentions truly are."

Chandler smiled. "Thanks for your vote of confidence."

"You bet," said MaryAnn, smiling. "And besides, if he is genuine and not involved in the revitalization, then maybe you will start dating."

"That brings up another sticky issue," Chandler said, wrinkling her nose. "What happens if it doesn't work out?"

"But what happens if it does?" MaryAnn asked with a smile. "I would love having you in the family."

MaryAnn finished the last of her coffee, looked at her watch, and said she'd better get back to the shop. "We were swamped yesterday about this time, and today it's just Rosie, Candy, and me."

Chandler gave her a hug and thanked her for the advice. After MaryAnn left, Chandler took her dishes back to the sink, and went to the office to return Peter's call. They agreed the best time to meet for the tour would be the following Thursday at 1:00 p.m., when bakery business slowed down for the day. Hanging up, she got back to work.

Chapter 13

"During the Civil War, Hope Springs was one of those towns that sustained minimal damage. Most of the fighting occurred outside the town limits. As a result, many of our downtown buildings are pre-Civil War," Chandler explained to Peter during their tour of the library the following Thursday. "The Hope Springs Library was one of the original structures erected in the late 1700s as the area was being colonized. It used to be a law office with a large library. As you can see, many of the wall shelves are original as are the tables in the non-fiction section. When you walk on the wooden floors you can almost sense the history here. Of course, there have been additions where the children's and technology sections are."

Peter took a lot of time to look past the books and tables to the structure itself. Except for a few windows that could use some work, the building looked to be in pretty good shape. He would love to have one of his structural engineers take a look, but wasn't sure how he could accomplish that without arousing suspicion.

"It's amazing to think about all the people who have walked through these rooms before us," Peter said in genuine awe. "It makes me wish I'd paid way more attention in history class."

"Town history has become something of a passion of mine," explained Chandler, "especially with the loss of my parents and grandparents. They all grew up here, so this is my heritage. Come to think of it, I guess it is yours as well," Chandler said, looking directly at him.

"Yes," Peter replied, somewhat surprised by that revelation. "I hadn't really thought about that."

As they walked next door to the Sweet Stuff Bakery, Peter once again looked closely at the structure. "Before this was a bakery, what was this building used for?" he asked, noticing the outside was definitely in need of some tender loving care.

"Believe it or not, this was the town Inn. The upper floors were rooms rented out by the night to weary travelers," Chandler explained as they entered the bakery. "They could come down here for coffee and a hearty breakfast before continuing their journey."

"Interesting," commented Peter as he looked around the interior. "What's upstairs now?"

"The owner of the building has converted it into two, one-bedroom apartments. Fortunately for me, that helps keep my rent low. Unfortunately for me, the landlord doesn't really want to invest in things that will keep the structure itself sound." Chandler walked over by the case containing display cakes. "If you stand here, you can feel the floor starting to give a little. I've spoken to him about it, but he doesn't seem too interested in fixing it anytime soon."

"Wouldn't that be a liability issue if someone were to fall because the floor gave way?" Peter asked, testing the stability of the floor.

"The landlord claims that it would be my fault since it is my shop. I've tried explaining to him that the law wouldn't see it that way, but he's a stubborn old man," Chandler said. "I've checked with my insurance, and luckily my liability insurance would cover it if the injured person were a customer. At the same time, that would also jack up my rates if I had to file a claim, and they are already higher than I want to pay. I'm trying to decide if it would be cheaper in the long run if I just fixed it myself."

"I noticed that the outside is looking a little weathered as well. I'm guessing the landlord isn't into curb appeal either," Peter stated, pointing toward the front of the store.

"Nope, I definitely depend on my signage and reputation to bring in customers," Chandler said. "Fortunately, I have more business that I can handle most of the time. Would you like a cup of coffee and something to eat? On the house," Chandler said with a smile.

"That sounds great," Peter said, realizing he was really enjoying his time with Chandler. He found it refreshing to have a conversation with a woman who wasn't looking for more than just conversation.
Looking at what was left in the case, Chandler asked, "Would you like a cheese Danish or a cinnamon roll?"

"A cinnamon roll would be wonderful," Peter answered enthusiastically. The smell of cinnamon had his mouth watering as soon as they had walked through the door.

"Have a seat and I'll be right back." Chandler went behind the counter to fix a tray with two cups of coffee and two of her best cinnamon rolls.

"He's cute," Gretchen whispered as Chandler added a small pitcher of cream, in case he didn't take his coffee black.

"Oh, stop," Chandler replied, looking over the front counter at her guest. "He's just here for the tour." Since the tables were already set with an assortment of sweeteners and silverware, she didn't need to grab those.

"Uh huh," Gretchen answered sarcastically.

While Chandler was getting the tray ready, Peter took the opportunity to take a closer look at the weakening floor. He snapped a few pictures, telling her he had a contractor friend who could see what needed to be done to shore up the floor.

"Does he do pro bono work?" asked Chandler, setting the tray on the table. "My budget is so tight, it squeaks as it is."

"I know his daughter is getting married in the fall, so maybe you can barter. He fixes your floor and you make her wedding cake," Peter suggested.

"I'm all for bartering," Chandler said with a smile. "Depending on the size of the cake, that might work."

Peter sipped his coffee, took a bite of the very big cinnamon roll she set before him, and smiled. "This is by far the best cinnamon roll I've had in a long time. And the coffee is equally delicious."

"Thank you," said Chandler. "Gretchen takes care of all of our baking for the morning crowd. She's here by 6:00 in the morning to get all the breakfast goodies ready for our 9:00 a.m. opening."

"So, it's just the two of you doing all the work?" asked Peter, looking around. The front of the bakery was large enough for four round tables, each with four chairs. All were adorned with cloth placemats, napkins, and silverware. He noticed that each also had a small centerpiece and assorted sweeteners. The whole place had a very casual, homey feel.

"No, Myrtle's granddaughter, Luann, just started working here for the summer," answered Chandler. "She's majoring in hotel and restaurant management. She'll be graduating next year and is interested in opening a bed and breakfast here in Hope Springs once she graduates."

"So what will you do when she goes back to college?" asked Peter, taking the last bite of his cinnamon roll.

"Hopefully there will be some local high school kids who will be looking for part-time employment then," she explained. "I was approached by a few last year, but I wasn't financially ready to hire more help. I'm hoping that won't be an issue this year."

Peter drank the last of his coffee and looked at his watch. "Darn," he said, "I need to get back to the city for a meeting."

Chandler got up and took their tray of dirty dishes to the counter. "Maybe you could come back another time so we can continue our tour? There are plenty of other buildings I'd love to tell you about."

"I'd like that a lot," Peter said, realizing he meant it. He smiled and continued, "I've had a great time today, and I'm glad you were able to get your hands out of the dough long enough to give me the tour."

Chandler smiled at his reference to her answering machine. "Next time we'll have to time it so we can go to the Hope Springs Diner for lunch. Andrea is an amazing cook. She shares her building with Rosie, and there's a lot of history there as well."

"I'll check my schedule for later next week and get back to you," Peter offered as he headed toward the door.

"Sounds good," Chandler agreed. She watched him walk toward his car, noticing that Myrtle and Fran were across the way sitting on one of the many benches that lined Main Street. *Oh, great,* she thought as she waved to them. *They'll be burning up the phone line by dinner time.* Then she remembered it was Thursday, and she'd be seeing them all later that evening. *I wonder if I can get out of going,* she thought. *No, they'd probably come and get me if I didn't show up. I might was well get it over with so I can get on with the rest of the week.*

Myrtle waved back, and turned to Fran. "It looks like they had a good, long visit," she said with a big smile. "Tonight's Advice Quilting Bee should be interesting."

"Yes, it should," said Fran, knowing that Myrtle would show no mercy.

Chapter 14

Myrtle came into the quilt shop smiling from ear to ear. "Good afternoon, ladies!" she shouted from the door. "I do believe love is in the air."

"Myrtle, must you be so loud?" Rosie admonished. She had been busy helping a customer and about jumped out of her skin. "And just why do you believe love is in the air?"

"Well," said Myrtle, fluffing up her curly, red hair, "because I just saw your grandson saying goodbye to our resident baker a few minutes ago, and they both had big smiles on their faces." As she marched down the center aisle, heels tapping with every step, Myrtle continued, "In fact, now that I think about it, I haven't seen Chandler smile like that in a long time."

"Will that be all, Nancy?" Rosie asked her customer. She really didn't want to have this conversation in front of one of her best customers. After Nancy nodded her head affirmatively, Rosie took her to the register to finish the transaction. Once Nancy left the store, Rosie turned to Myrtle. "I thought Chandler was just giving Peter a tour of Hope Springs?"

"That was what today was supposed to be about, but she invited him back to the bakery for a treat before he left. They were both smiling when she walked him out the door," said Myrtle with a knowing smirk.

"Before we have them walking down the aisle, why don't we reserve judgment until we talk to Chandler. She'll be here tonight," said Rosie. As much as she wanted her grandson to find someone, and as much as she would love for that someone to be Chandler, she didn't want to put the cart before the horse.

"Don't you worry, Rosie. I'm definitely going to get all the details," Myrtle said, rubbing her hands together like the evil villain in a horror movie.

"Oh, brother," Rosie groaned. "Since you're here so early, would you mind getting the back room ready for tonight? I'd like to take a little break and MaryAnn is watching the front," said Rosie.

"No problem," Myrtle assured her. "You go rest and I'll take care of everything."

Fortunately, the rest of the day was pretty quiet so the ladies could get ready for their Thursday night Advice Quilting Bee. Once everyone was there, they had dinner and got busy working on the quilt. There were only a few more rows to go before it would be ready to come off of the frame.

"Okay, ladies," said Rosie, "We are close to being done with this one. If we buckle down tonight, we just might get it finished."

"So, is anything interesting going on in anyone's life?" asked Myrtle, shooting a pointed glance at Chandler.

Chandler kept her eyes on her needle, thinking maybe Myrtle would ask someone else if she ignored her, but she could sense all the eyes looking her direction. *So much for keeping things quiet in a small town,* she thought. "Not me," she said, "aside from graduation cakes, things have been pretty quiet at the bakery." That brought a few snickers from the crowd, since they all knew Myrtle wouldn't be content with that answer.

"Well," said Myrtle, "I noticed you going around town with Rosie's grandson today. He seemed to spend quite a bit of time at your bakery before he left."

"Oh, that," Chandler said somewhat sarcastically. "Don't you remember, Myrtle? You wanted me to give him a tour of our town and teach him all about the history. Well, that's exactly what I did."

"Why was he at the bakery for so long?" Myrtle asked, pulling her reading glasses off her nose.

"Myrtle, did you have spies watching our every move?" asked Chandler, suspiciously. She had seen Myrtle and Fran sitting on the bench when Peter left and knew this conversation would be coming. Chandler loved teasing Myrtle about what she liked to call the Little Old Lady Network. She had seen it in action before. Myrtle and about three or four other ladies, Fran included, followed people around town, and would report back to the group their observations.

Myrtle put her hand to her chest. "Chandler, I'm hurt that you would think such a thing. Fran and I were sitting on one of the benches in front of the diner just enjoying our day. We saw you two go into the bakery and come out about forty-five minutes later. How much history is there to teach him about one shop?"

Chandler's jaw dropped. "Just what do you think we were doing in there?" That brought another round of snickers from the rest of the group. "Not that it's anyone's business," she explained, "but we were having pastries and coffee and I was telling him more of the history of the town."

Fran took this moment to try to get Myrtle out of trouble. "Chandler, we weren't spying on you. Myrtle is genuinely concerned about you and wants to see you happy."

"Fran, you're a true friend," said Chandler, smiling. "Myrtle, I know you're concerned about me, but I'd like to handle things my way. If it makes you feel any better, we are going to get together again soon to finish our tour." Chandler wasn't sure if she should share this bit of information, but maybe they would finally drop the interrogation and move on to someone else.

Unfortunately, Rosie took this opportunity to say, "That's wonderful, dear. Peter would do very well to have someone like you in his life."

Chandler tried not to cringe. She didn't want to get Rosie's hopes up, and still wasn't sure if she actually wanted anything to come of whatever this was between them. "Well, let's just take this one visit at a time, shall we?" She picked up her needle and went back to quilting, praying someone else would change the subject. MaryAnn chimed in, coming to her rescue.

"Luann, how do you like working at the bakery?" asked MaryAnn, as she continued stitching her row.

"For the few days I've been there, I love it," Luann said with a smile, tucking her shoulder length, brown hair behind one ear. "Gretchen and Chandler are teaching me so much about running the business, and I'm learning some great baking skills. To be honest, though, once I open my own bed and breakfast, I'll probably get all my baked goods from them. The entrepreneur in me says that would be great advertising for us both."

"I think that's a great idea," said MaryAnn. "Have you been scoping out potential properties for your bed and breakfast?"

"I've looked around a little," replied Luann, "but since I still have another year of college, I'm not quite ready to make the leap yet."

"That will be so exciting for Hope Springs," said MaryAnn, looking up and smiling. "When it comes time to secure your financing, let me know. I can put in a good word with the Hope Springs Bank president."

"Thanks," said Luann. "I'm sure I'm also going to need an accountant. Hillary, do you think Jack would be interested in taking on a new client?"

"If he knows what's good for him at home, he will," Hillary said, laughing as she attempted to thread her needle. "He may know of a contractor as well. When the time comes, let me know and I'll ask him."

"I guess this is one of the many perks of living in a small town," said Luann, smiling. "Everyone knows someone they can recommend for just about anything."

"Macy, have things quieted down at the medical center?" asked Rosie, finishing the row of stitching she was working on. "I remember when we last spoke, you were pretty busy with sick children." After securing the knot at the end, she clipped the thread with a small pair of scissors she had pinned to her apron.

"Yes, thank goodness that's over," said Macy, looking up from her own work. "Dr. Howard said if we had another week like the last one, he just might retire sooner than he planned."

Rosie took off her reading glasses. "He's thinking of retiring?" she asked, concerned. "That would be a big loss for the town. He has been the town doctor for so long."

"Yes," answered Macy, somewhat sadly. "I agree it would be a loss, but he said he wants to play golf while he's still able to walk the course and see from the tee to the green. It sounds like it could be within the next year."

"Well, he is getting up there in years," said Myrtle. "Besides, maybe they will replace him with some hot, young doctor!"

"Myrtle!" exclaimed Rosie. "That is not any way to talk at your age."

"Oh, Rosie," Myrtle sighed, "stop being a fuddy-duddy. It might be good to have something nice to look at when you're sick."

"My, oh my," Fran said, shaking her head. "Is this what our generation has come to?" She turned to talk to the younger members of the group. "Please promise me that when you are our age, you won't act like this. Age gracefully, but not too gracefully, if you know what I mean."

Chandler smiled. "We know what you mean, Fran. You want us to be more like you, somewhere between Rosie and Myrtle."

"Exactly!" smiled Fran, straightening her peasant blouse over one shoulder.

"Alright, back to the quilt," said Rosie. "How are we doing?"

MaryAnn looked it over, "I do believe that we are ready to do the last turn of the quilt. We have done a lot this evening, but we have also done a lot of talking. It's almost 10:00, so I think we have one more week to go."

Everyone agreed and decided that maybe next week there should be more working and less talking. Somehow, Chandler had a hunch that if she met with Peter again before then, the quilt would have to wait yet another week.

Chapter 15

"I'm glad you like the idea of a barter for your daughter's wedding cake," Peter said into the phone on Monday morning. Chuck Marshall had been happy to help Peter with his undercover fact-finding mission when he learned it could help with wedding costs. "I'd like you to take a look at the floor of the bakery as well as the entire structure of the building, while you're there." Peter could hear Chuck quickly taking notes in the background as he laid out the details of his request. "While you're at it," Peter continued, "see if you can visit the library, visitor's center, and post office as well. I'd really hate to tear them down if we could feasibly enhance them."

"No problem, boss," Chuck said as he finished making notes. "My daughter is a big history buff. She's always talking about wanting to get out of the city and see some of the small historical towns in Virginia. We'll set up an appointment with the bakery lady and let you know how it goes."

"I'd like to get this done within the week, so I'll talk to her first and give her your number. I'll see if she is available Saturday morning so you can make a day of historical sightseeing out of it." Peter really wanted this information before Cassia made her next move, and he wasn't sure how long he could hold her off.

"Sounds good. Just let me know what's what," Chuck answered.

"I'll ask Chandler to call you to confirm for Saturday. Thanks again for doing this." Peter said goodbye and hung up. His next call was to Chandler.

Chandler was just pulling a fresh batch of cookies out of the big commercial oven when the phone rang. "I'll get it," she yelled to Gretchen, who was in the storage room in the back of the building. Chandler reached up to answer the phone, "Sweet Stuff Bakery, Chandler speaking."

Peter smiled at the sound of her voice. "Glad I caught you between graduation cakes."

Chandler smiled. "Hi, Peter, what's up?" she asked, trying not to think about why her stomach just did a summersault.

"Do you remember that business proposition we discussed?" he asked.

"You mean the one involving my floor getting fixed in exchange for a wedding cake?" she surmised.

"That's the one," he confirmed. "When I spoke to my engineer, Chuck Marshall, he was very interested in doing a little bartering with you for his daughter's wedding cake. I could give you his number if you'd like to set up a meeting. He was wondering if he and his daughter could come down this Saturday to meet with you about the cake and take a look at the floor."

"Okay, let me grab a pen and get this number," Chandler said, reaching into the Sweet Stuff Bakery cup she kept near the phone. She put the phone under her chin so she'd have both hands free. "You said his name was Chuck, right?"

"Yes, and his number is 555-384-8965," Peter said. "He'll be expecting your call."

Chandler had hoped Peter was calling to see when they could continue their history tour, but she quickly switched gears. "I'll call him as soon as we're done here. I can definitely meet with them this Saturday. Every time someone stands near that display case, I get a little worried. The sooner I can get that taken care of, the better."

"Wonderful," Peter said, smiling. "While I have you on the phone, do you have time this week to continue our history tour? I believe you mentioned something last Thursday about planning it around lunch at the Hope Springs Diner."

This made Chandler smile. "Yes I do! Friday I'll be busy getting cakes ready for the weekend. What is your schedule like on Thursday?" she asked, looking at her calendar.

As Peter looked, he saw that his calendar was packed, but replied, "All clear. What time is good for you?"

"How about if we meet at the bakery around 10:00 that morning?" she suggested. "The breakfast crowd will have dispersed by then. We can do our tour and then end with lunch?"

"That works for me," said Peter, making a note to have Pat clear his calendar. "I'll see you then."

They hung up after wishing each other a good week, both smiling at the prospect of seeing the other. Chandler turned to see that Gretchen was crumb-coating a sheet cake. Crumb coating was an important step in getting a cake ready for decorating. It involved leveling the top with a long serrated knife, brushing loose crumbs off and spreading a thin layer of buttercream frosting over the entire cake. Then it was placed in the refrigerator to firm up. As every good baker knew, a good crumb coat was essential to a beautifully decorated cake.

Gretchen looked up from the cake she was working on. "So, you're meeting Rosie's grandson again?" she asked, smiling.

Chandler gave her a sideways glance. "Yes, and I'd really appreciate it if the Little Old Lady Network didn't find out."

"Oh, you mean Myrtle and her friends?" Gretchen asked, knowing exactly who she meant.

"Who else do you know who goes around town in a little pack with their pocketbooks on their arms? Honestly, the hazards of living in a small town," Chandler said, shaking her head.

"Just checking. I love that you've given them a name. The Little Old Lady Network is certainly fitting," said Gretchen with a smile. "You know they're just living vicariously through you because they know they're past their prime," she added, defending the group.

"I suppose," Chandler said. Wanting to change the subject, she turned to the stack of orders for cakes, asking, "Where are we on the baking for all these orders? I'd like to get the sheets baked and crumb-coated so they're ready for a marathon decorating session on Friday." She looked through the stack, saying "I'm so glad Luann will be able to work all this week. We're going to need the extra help."

"We'll have the sheets ready to go," Gretchen reassured her. "Luckily, they're all graduation cakes, so it's pretty much simple decorations and names at this point. There are a couple of customers who ordered photos on their cakes, and I'll make sure they're ready by Friday." She picked up the cake she'd been working on and headed for the large refrigerator. "It really helps having Luann do customer service so I can stay back here and get everything else done. If we need to stay late to finish, I'm available and so is Luann."

"You guys are the best," smiled Chandler. "It's so nice to have a staff that I feel comfortable leaving for a few hours, knowing the bakery isn't going to burn down."

"Anything to help your developing love life," Gretchen said teasingly.

"Ha!" laughed Chandler. "Let's just get back to work and maybe get out of here at a decent hour today. It's only Monday, but there's still a lot to accomplish this week."

The rest of the day went by in a blur. They had a big rush around 2:00 p.m. with folks wanting an afternoon sweet to get them through the rest of the day. By 4:00 p.m., everything was pretty much sold out. By closing time at 5:00 p.m., all orders that needed to be picked up had been, and they were boxing up a few leftover pastries and cookies to be dropped off at the fire department. Luann said she'd make that delivery. Gretchen offered to stay and help Chandler clean the remaining pans, but Chandler pushed her out the door since she had been the first to arrive at 6:00 in the morning.

By 6:00 p.m., everything was good to go for the next day, so Chandler turned off the lights and locked the front door on her way out. Standing in front of her shop, she looked around her small town. Taking a deep breath, Chandler loved the fact that she could smell the flowers in the boxes on the sidewalk instead of car exhaust. The sun was just starting to go behind her shop, leaving the sidewalk in front shaded. The air was still warm, but not so stifling that it was too hot to walk. And she could feel a bit of a breeze coming from the lake on the south edge of town.

Chandler loved the fact that she didn't have to put bars on her doors and windows, and knew the bakery would be safe once she left for the night. And as annoying as the Little Old Lady Network could be, she still loved them and this town. She walked up the sidewalk two blocks to the Hope Springs Bank and put her night deposit in the drop box.

Chandler started to turn to cross Main Street toward home, but decided to turn the other way and take a walk around the historic district where the grand old homes stood. She passed by Myrtle's house and continued toward Rosie's. She looked up at the house and saw that Rosie was sitting on the veranda. While Chandler's home was small, Rosie's was much larger. Chandler knew that Rosie's ancestors had built the home, and that Rosie was very proud to have been able to keep it in her family.

Rosie stood and waved. "Good evening, Chandler. Can I interest you in a glass of sweet tea?" she asked.

Chandler knew that Rosie made some of the best and sweetest tea in town, so she couldn't resist. "I'd love to join you. It's such a beautiful evening to waste sitting inside," she answered walking up past Rosie's beautiful gardens to the front porch. The smell was as heavenly as it was on Main Street.

As they settled in with their tea, Rosie inquired, "How is business at the bakery?"

"Since graduation season and wedding season coincide, we're always busy at this time f the year. I'm glad to have Gretchen, and now Luann, helping me get everything done on time," Chandler replied after taking a sip of her tea. "Rosie, you do make the best sweet tea around," she declared.

Rosie smiled. "Thank you dear, but I do hope that you still have time for a social life. That's so important for someone your age. You don't want to spend all your time working and have no one special in your life." Rosie worried about the younger women in her group. Aside from Hillary, who had a family already, the others were all single and running their businesses almost single-handedly.

Chandler thought about that and decided maybe now was the time to talk to Rosie about Peter. She really didn't want to have this conversation in front of everyone at the Advice Quilting Bee.

"Rosie, as a matter of fact, Peter's coming on Thursday to continue our history tour and to have lunch at the diner," she announced. She was still leery about anything more than this being a history tour. She didn't know Peter aside from what she'd learned from having spent a couple hours with him. And the whole thing about him being a developer unnerved her. But, as Myrtle had said before, the only way to see what he was up to was to spend time with him.

Rosie took a sip of her tea and placed her glass on the white wicker table next to her matching rocking chair. She, too, sensed Chandler's hesitation. Rosie had been around long enough to be able to read a person's body language, and Chandler definitely had reservations about Peter. "I think that's wonderful, Chandler," she said, trying to let Chandler know she approved. "It would do Peter some good to get out of that big city his mother dragged him to all those years ago, and see where his roots are."

This was the first time Chandler ever remembered Rosie addressing her daughter leaving Hope Springs. "Rosie, you know my history and how my parents died. Family is so important to me. I'm just surprised you hadn't seen Peter in so long. Do you know why he hadn't visited before now?"

Rosie fluffed her white hair and smoothed the hem of her top over her lap. "I think Ramona didn't paint a very pretty picture of our small town when he was growing up. Once he was old enough to make his own choices, I continued to see him for the holidays, but he was driven to make his company a success. Then, when she died, I think he wasn't sure how to reach out to us. I guess I'm just so glad he had business in the area that brought him back here."

"Rosie, could you see Peter settling down here in Hope Springs?" Chandler asked. She always valued Rosie's opinions.

"Well, my Charles was here working at the bank, on loan from the main offices in the city, when we met," Rosie answered. "I wasn't sure he would like to stay here, but he did. Love will do that to you; make you realize what is most important in your life."

Chandler still had her doubts about Peter's story, but she didn't want to burden Rosie with that. Instead, she addressed the other doubt weighing on her mind. "Rosie, I'm not saying that this is going to happen, but how would you feel if Peter and I did start dating?"

Rosie smiled. "Chandler, I think you're just what Peter needs, and I would support you wholeheartedly."

"My concern," Chandler paused, taking a sip of her tea, "is, what if it doesn't work out? I would hate for that to change the relationship I have with you."

Rosie reached over and took Chandler's hand. "My dear, whatever happens between you and my grandson, you and I will always have a very special relationship. Nothing will change that."

"How can you be so sure?" Chandler asked, concern on her face.

Rosie smiled. "Eighty-three years of experience tells me that if it doesn't work out, it will be his fault, not yours!" Both women laughed at that.

"Well, I'd say that I'll keep you posted," Chandler said, picking up her glass, "but something tells me Myrtle will get to you before I will." She finished her tea and set the glass on the table.

Rosie shook her head from side to side, "Yes, I suspect you're right about that. Myrtle, Fran and her little group do seem to have their finger on the pulse of what's happening in Hope Springs."

"Rosie, I've dubbed them the Little Old Lady Network," Chandler said, laughing. "They have spies all over town!"

"I know they do. I think they've even conned some of the older gentlemen in our community to join them," Rosie agreed.

"Well, at least we know that if anything bad happens in Hope Springs, there will be lots of eye witnesses," Chandler concluded.

They visited a little while longer before Chandler decided she best continue on before it got too dark. She knew the next day would be another busy one, and she would need get a good night's sleep.

As Chandler continued her walk around the historic district, she looked at some of the homes that might be potential bed and breakfasts for Luann. Many of the homes had already been restored, but there were still a good number from which to choose. Of course, it would depend on Luann's timeline, budget, and home availability, but Chandler thought Luann definitely had the determination and business know-how to get it done.

Walking down the street to her own home, Chandler considered what it would be like to live in the historic district. She knew that she'd probably be able to sell her cottage for a fair price and move to the other side of Main Street. However, she'd probably need to purchase a fixer upper, and she didn't have the time or the resources to tackle that kind of renovation. She decided that she loved where she grew up, especially since she had spent so much time restoring it, and she was happy just where she was.

Chapter 16

Peter looked at his ringing cell phone and saw that it was Cassia. She was one of the meetings he had Pat change when he asked her to clear his calendar, so he was sure she was calling about that. He really didn't want to deal with her today. Today was Thursday, and he was going to be seeing Chandler. He still wasn't ready to admit that the thought of seeing her again did weird things to his stomach. She wasn't like any of the women he usually dated, but none of those women made him feel the way she did.

In the small amount of time he'd spent with Chandler, Peter felt it wasn't necessary to be the big shot developer he was known to be here in the city. She had no idea how profitable his company was, and she didn't seem the type to care about how much money he had in his bank account. Peter didn't realize he wanted a woman like that until he'd met Chandler Bradford.

He let the call go to voicemail and thought back to a conversation he'd had with Jake that morning at the gym. Jake had asked him if he could think of any of the women he recently dated that he would like to see again. For the life of him, he hadn't even been able to remember some of their names. Jake said that alone spoke volumes. All he knew was that he was looking forward to spending the morning with Chandler and having lunch afterwards.

Peter looked at the clock and decided he could forgo the office and go straight to Hope Springs to avoid the possibility of running into Cassia. He also decided he could go casual as well, and changed from his suit and tie to jeans and a short-sleeved polo. He looked in the mirror and realized he was hoping Chandler would approve. Man, he really did have it bad. Grabbing his sunglasses and keys he headed out the door. He stepped out of the elevator and ran right into Cassia.

"Oh!" a startled Cassia said. "Peter, I was just coming to see you. You didn't answer your phone and Pat cancelled our meeting, so I thought maybe you were sick. I was coming to take care of you." Then she stopped talking long enough to look him up and down. "But I see now that you are perfectly healthy and not dressed for work at all. Just where are you headed dressed like that?"

He decided to be honest with her, almost. "I'm heading to Hope Springs to spend some time with my grandmother," he said as he tried to keep walking toward the door.

"I'd love to meet your grandmother," Cassia said excitedly. "Why don't I come along?"

Over Cassia's shoulder, Peter noticed Carl watching intently from his security desk. Peter scowled at him for not warning him Cassia was in the building. Carl just smiled and shrugged his shoulders.

"Peter," Cassia whined impatiently, "you haven't answered my question. May I come along?"

Peter put his hand on her arm. "You know, as nice as that sounds, I would really want to speak with her ahead of time to let her know you're coming. If there's one thing my grandmother taught me years ago, it's that southern ladies do not like visitors to arrive unannounced." It was a blatant lie; southern ladies loved drop-in guests. Cassia's only experience with southern ladies, however, was probably "Gone with the Wind".

Cassia smiled, a little. "How sweet, southern charm alive and well. Have a good visit with your grandmother, then," she said, patting his arm with her manicured hand. "I think Pat rescheduled our meeting for Tuesday, but I'm free all weekend," she said suggestively.

Peter knew a come-on when he heard one. "I'll keep that in mind, but I already have plans with Jake to go to the ball games Saturday and Sunday. It's nice to have someone with connections to box seats. Have a great weekend," he said, practically pushing her out the door.

"Okay," Cassia said dejectedly. "You have a good weekend, too."

After he was sure she was out the door, Peter turned toward Carl, who had really been enjoying the show. "Okay, Carl, next time she comes in the building, you better let me know immediately," Peter said, shaking his finger at the doorman.

"I'm sorry, Mr. Frederick," Carl said with his hands up in front of him. "I swear I tried to stop her, but she hurried right past. Then the elevator opened and there you were. By the way, nice save on why you're dressed like that."

"What do you mean nice save?"

Carl laughed, "Oh, come on now. You and I both know you're not dressed like that to go to Hope Springs to have lunch with your grandmother. I'm guessing you're having lunch with the young lady you and I had the conversation about the other night."

Peter's mouth dropped open. "How did you know?"

"I've been around a long time, Mr. Frederick, and I've seen and heard it all. But my advice to you is that you better at least go and visit your grandmother so your story is somewhat legitimate, or that little blonde will come after you," he said, smiling and pointing to the door.

Peter put his sunglasses on. "Have a good day, Carl," he said with a smile.

"You have a good day, too, Mr. Frederick," Carl smiled back.

Chapter 17

Peter pulled up in front of the bakery. As he got out of his car he noticed Myrtle, Fran and another lady he didn't recognize walking up the sidewalk. "Good morning! How are you lovely, young ladies doing this morning?" he asked flashing a bright, white smile.

Myrtle, who was clearly the spokeswoman for the group, smiled. "Good morning, Mr. Frederick. What brings you to Hope Springs on this beautiful day?" As if she had to ask.

"Well, I've come to kidnap your local baker to make her show me more of your town," Peter said. He knew she was fishing for gossip.

"Oh, how wonderful!" exclaimed Myrtle. "You know, I saw her this morning and noticed she has her hair and makeup done today. That must be why, she knew you were coming. I see you're dressed quite handsomely as well. If I didn't know better, Mr. Frederick, I'd say you are coming to take our Chandler out on a date."

"Now, Myrtle," Fran cautioned, "don't go storytelling when there isn't a story to tell."

Myrtle shushed Fran. "But there may be. Right, Mr. Frederick?" she asked, smiling.

"Well, if your story is that Chandler is continuing our tour of the city, then I guess there is one. Really, though, that doesn't sound too exciting to me," Peter said, thinking that this conversation was kind of fun. He'd never experienced this type of small-town know-it-all before. Obviously, Myrtle was the proverbial town crier.

"Okay, Myrtle, how about if we let Mr. Frederick get on with his day," said Fran, trying to usher Myrtle along. Peter guessed Fran was the voice of reason. And he still didn't know the other woman's name, but guessed she was just along for the ride.

"Yes, yes, of course," Myrtle smiled. "We hope you have a great visit today, Mr. Frederick. Be sure to enjoy the *sights,*" she finished with a wink.

Peter smiled. "Have a wonderful day, ladies. And, please, call me Peter."

"Peter, then," said Myrtle. The three ladies waved goodbye and headed down the street toward the crosswalk most likely they were headed to Rosie's to announce his arrival.

Chandler had seen the entire exchange from behind the counter in the bakery. *Lord only knows what the Little Old Lady Network is up to,* she thought with a shake of her head. She had to admit, though, it did give her a chance to get a good look at Peter without him knowing. Boy, he was good looking! She thought he looked wonderful in a suit and tie, but dressed in a light blue polo and jeans, he was drop dead gorgeous. By the way everything fit, she could definitely tell he worked out. A lot!

"Wow," Luann whispered loudly over Chandler's shoulder. "He looks even better in jeans and a polo shirt than he did in a suit."

"Yep," said Gretchen, smiling, "and he has his sights set on our Chandler."

"Lucky you," said Luann. "My Grandma Myrtle told me she thought you and Rosie's grandson would make a cute couple. I can see that she was right."

"Oh, now stop, you two," scolded Chandler. "We're just finishing our tour of the town and having lunch at the diner. Nothing more."

"Really," said Gretchen, "because I've worked with you since the bakery opened, and I don't think I've ever seen you come to work with makeup on and your hair in anything other than a ponytail."

"I just decided to try something new today," lied Chandler, smoothing her hand over her hair. "Now hush up and go back to work because he's coming in."

"Good morning, ladies," Peter said, bursting through the front door a few moments later. "It smells absolutely heavenly in here."

"Hi," said Chandler, smiling. "It's the cinnamon rolls. Would you like one?"

"I'd love one, but I've heard the Hope Springs Diner has the best chocolate cream pie in town, and I want to make sure I have room," Peter said, rubbing his belly. "I ran into Myrtle and her posse on my way in, so I'm guessing half the town knows I'm here by now."

"Oh, you mean the Little Old Lady Network?" asked Gretchen.

"The *what*?" Peter asked curiously.

"That's what Chandler calls them," explained Gretchen. "You never see just one of them, and whenever they have news, it gets all over town in five minutes flat. Much better than social media."

"Well, maybe we should start our tour by making a stop at Rosie's since I think that's where they were headed," Peter said, pointing over his shoulder toward Rosie's shop.

"You two kids have fun, and don't worry about the bakery," said Gretchen, a big smile on her usually serious face. "Luann and I have everything under control."

"Thanks," Chandler said with a hint of a glare toward Gretchen. "We'll be back after lunch." *Good lord,* Chandler thought, *even Gretchen is in the matchmaking business.*

"Take your time," Chandler heard Gretchen say as they headed out the door.

Once they were out of earshot, Peter said, "I like your hair down like this; it really suits you."

Chandler smiled. "Well, this will raise a lot of eyebrows as well, because hardly anyone has seen me wear it like this. It gets in the way when I'm working."

"Why did you decide to wear it that way today?" Peter asked.

Chandler dodged the question. "I could ask you the same question. I've only seen you in a suit and tie."

Peter smiled, "I guess we both thought it was time for something new."

Chandler decided that was a good sign. She really was tired of the same old routine every day, even if she was sure this would just give the ladies of the Advice Quilting Bee more to talk about.

Chandler wasn't sure where this thing with Peter was headed, but she was certainly on board with finding out.

As they were getting ready to cross the street, Peter asked, "Do you mind if we invite my grandmother to lunch? Not that I don't want to spend as much time with you as possible, but I'd like to spend some time with her as well."

Chandler smiled. "I was actually going to ask you if you'd like to do that." She really didn't mind sharing her time, and was so happy to hear they both had the same idea.

"Oh," Chandler said, "I spoke with Chuck and I am meeting him and his daughter Saturday morning at 9:00. He said she's into small town history and wants to check out some of our historic buildings while they're here."

"Good, I'm glad they're coming so soon. The sooner you can get your floor fixed, the better." *And the sooner Chuck checks everything out and takes pictures to report back to me, the better*, he thought. Peter really wanted to see if there was any way to save the buildings and reconfigure the design.

Chandler led the way into Rosie's Quilting Emporium. Since it was Thursday, she knew both Rosie and MaryAnn would be there getting ready for the Advice Quilting Bee meeting tonight. However, as they walked through the door, they ran smack dab into the Little Old Lady Network.

"Oh!" exclaimed Myrtle. "I didn't expect to see you in here before tonight, Chandler."

"Hello, Myrtle," said Chandler, looking past her to see who she'd brought with her. "Hello, Fran, Mabel" she finished with a nod to each. "How are both of you today?"

Mabel Clark was the first to speak. "I'm doing fine this morning, Chandler. It's been so long since I've seen you. Have you done something with your hair? It's absolutely lovely."

Chandler could hear Peter chuckling behind her, and had to fight the urge to nudge him with her elbow. "Yes, Mabel, I decided to leave it down today instead of my usual ponytail," she said with her best dear, sweet, nosy, old lady smile.

"Well, you should wear it that way every day," Mabel said. "Don't you agree Peter?"

Subtlety isn't their strong suit, thought Peter. "Yes, I agree," he said, smiling. *These ladies really are something else.*

"Unfortunately, in my line of work I need to keep my hair up and out of the way," said Chandler. "You wouldn't want to eat baked goods with hair in them, would you?"

"Okay, ladies," said Fran as she was trying keep them moving out the door. "Let's let them get on with their day."

"We'll be seeing you here tonight, won't we, Chandler?" Myrtle asked.

Chandler smiled. "Of course you will, Myrtle." She knew there would be more grilling tonight than last week, for sure. "Don't forget that we're almost done with our quilt, so we really should do more stitching and less talking."

"Oh, don't worry, we will," Myrtle said patting Chandler's hand. "Now you both have a great day."

Peter held the door open for the three of them as they exited the store. "I'm sure we will," he said, smiling. "I'd say for you to have a lovely day, again, but something tells me we'll be seeing each other again soon." With that, he let the front door close and turned to see Chandler staring at him, smiling. "What?" he asked.

"Oh, nothing," she said. "It's just that I've never met a man so patient with them before. Most men I've known think they are very annoying and nosy."

"I actually find them quite entertaining," he laughed. "I definitely don't know anyone like them in the city, well, except Carl."

"Who's Carl?" asked Chandler.

"My doorman," answered Peter. "He's always interested in my private life. I guess you could call him a one man version of your Little Old Lady Network."

"I'm going to have to meet him someday, to compare of course," Chandler said, blushing a bit when she realized how presumptuous she sounded.

"I think that can be arranged," Peter said, quietly enough that none of Rosie's customers could hear. He could swear Chandler's cheeks flushed an even brighter shade of pink.

Chandler wasn't sure how to answer that. Was Peter just hinting about the possibility of them seeing each other for something other than a tour? If so, how did she feel about it? Luckily she was saved from trying to figure it out immediately when Rosie emerged from the back room.

"Chandler and Peter, what a nice surprise," she exclaimed. "Peter, what brings you back to Hope Springs so soon, as if I even need to ask?" She gave them each a hug, and Peter a wink.

Peter loved his grandmother for the understated way she was able to ask a question she clearly already had the answer to. "As

I'm sure you've already heard, Chandler and I are going to finish our tour of the town. Then we're going to the diner for lunch, and were wondering if we could talk you into joining us?"

"I'd love to, dear," she said excitedly, "but I don't want to intrude on your time together."

Chandler made sure Rosie understood that they both wanted her to join them. "Maybe if Peter has any questions about the town history that I can't answer, you could take care of that at lunch," she said.

"Well, then, it would be my pleasure," Rosie responded, looking at her watch. "The diner is usually crowded for lunch until around 1:00, and that's about the time things slow down in here. How about if you come back then, and we can walk over together?"

"Sounds like a plan," said Peter. "We'll see you then."

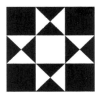

Chapter 18

Peter opened the door for Chandler to pass, and asked, "Which way today?" They'd already seen the library and her bakery. He really wanted to get a look at the post office and visitor's center. The building housing the CPA's office and boutique were the other structures on Cassia's hit list.

"Let's go toward the visitor's center first. There are some interesting stories associated with that building," Chandler said, leading the way. "When you look at the outside walls of the building, you can still see bullets lodged in the siding. The building used to be the courthouse. Apparently there was a gun battle during one trial and the prisoner escaped with the help of his brothers. Somehow no one was hurt, but there are bullets all over."

"Guess they were either really lucky or really lousy shots," Peter said, chuckling.

"The sheriff found out later that evening that the men had a run-in with another group of bandits about five miles outside of town. Six men in total were involved. The prisoner and his brothers were all killed and the others escaped into the night, never to be seen again. Rumor has it there have been sightings of the killed men in a few of the fields outside of town."

"You mean, like, ghosts?" asked Peter, disbelievingly.

"Oh, yeah, this town is full of them. You'll have to come back on a weekend night and we can do a ghost-walk tour. It's awesome!" Chandler said, smiling.

"Have you had encounters with ghosts?" Peter asked, very curious about the whole thing.

"No, but I do know others who have. I guess I'm not one of the lucky ones who get to experience that," she answered somewhat sad.

"Would you really like to?" he asked, a little amazed, considering how practical and down-to-earth Chandler seemed.

"I think it would be great if I had a visit from my parents or grandparents," she replied. "Though I'm not sure I'd want to see a bunch of bandit ghosts in the middle of a field!"

By now they were standing outside the visitor's center. "See, here are some of the bullets," Chandler said pointing to the old siding. "The building could really use a facelift, but no one wants to cover them up, so it still looks like this. A restoration team looked at the building and surmised that the only way to preserve it would be to remove each board, refinish them individually, and then return them to their original place on the wall. It would cost more money than the visitor's center or town has, so for now it looks like this."

They walked into the building, and Peter noticed that the inside looked much better than the outside. The floors were relatively level for a building a century and a half old, and felt pretty solid. This gave him hope.

"The woodwork in here is all original, just like the library. The community has taken great pains to preserve as much originality to each building as possible. Come this way and I'll show you the main courtroom. It has been transformed into an all-purpose room, housing everything from meetings to weddings," Chandler said.

"Guess a wedding in the judge's chambers is out of the question," commented Peter.

"Oh, yes," replied Chandler, "and when a wedding happens in here, the wedding party is usually dressed in period costumes. It's a really nice touch."

"Interesting. It seems that the folks in this town use every inch of space for its intended purpose, and then some," he surmised.

Just then they were joined by one of the women who volunteered at the visitor's center. Peter recognized her right away as Myrtle's friend, Mabel. "See, I knew we'd be seeing each other again soon," Peter said, shaking Mabel's hand.

"I'm so glad your tour brought you to the visitor's center, Peter. How much has Chandler told you about our building?" Mabel asked, still holding Peter's hand and grinning ear to ear.

Peter tried to extricate his hand, but she had a death grip on it. "Well, she told me all about how the bullets came to be lodged in the façade, and was just telling me how this room is currently being used for meetings and weddings."

Peter noticed Chandler laughing at the way Mabel was holding on to his hand for dear life. "Mabel, why don't you tell Peter a little more about the inside while I go and get him some of the brochures?"

Peter gave Chandler a look that clearly said, *"Please don't leave me alone with her,"* but he just stood there patiently listening as Mabel went on about different cases that had been tried in the courtroom. Peter noticed her stories weren't really of any historical significance, until she got to the one where a man was tried for

115

killing his wife's lover by throwing him in the thrashing machine at the Cotton Mill. "Wait a minute." He held up his free hand. "You mean to tell me someone was actually *murdered* in Hope Springs?"

"Oh, yes," Mabel went on to say, "it was quite the story. You see, after the wife found out what had happened, she killed herself because she couldn't bear to live without her lover anymore. Supposedly, they have been spotted together holding hands down by the lake."

"Another ghost story," Peter stated.

"One of the many," Chandler said, coming back from getting the brochures. "It's a stop on the ghost-walk tour as well."

"I'll definitely have to come back so we can take that tour. My curiosity is certainly piqued," Peter said, finally getting his hand free from Mabel.

He looked at Mabel and saw she had a very interested look on her face at his last statement. It was then that he knew she would be telling the Little Old Lady Network that he would be making a return trip to Hope Springs. He figured there was probably a back door to this place, and that as he and Chandler exited through the front, Mabel would be exiting out the back, to spread the word.

Chandler realized what had just happened as well. She just didn't know of a way to stop it. *Oh well*, she thought, *at least he is interested in coming back for another visit*. The more time she spent with Peter, the more she was beginning to realize he may have a little bit of small town life in him. While she still wasn't sure where this was going, it didn't seem as scary as before.

"Where else are you headed?" asked Mabel.

Chandler mentally noted that Mabel wasn't the best of spies. "Well, we're going to the post office next."

"Oh," Mabel said, as if visiting the post office wasn't a very exciting development for her to report. "Since it's getting close to lunch time, I hope you'll take Peter to the diner, Chandler."

Chandler smiled, "What an excellent suggestion, Mabel."

Chandler knew they would be seeing Mabel and her friends at the diner. They said their goodbyes to Mabel and made their way to the post office next door. "This building has always been the post office," Chandler said as they walked in the front door.

Peter noticed the outside looked much like the visitor's center, but the inside was completely updated. As he looked around, he saw that the walls were covered with photos of the old post office, and the inside had been refurbished with new wood paneling painted off white. This gave the walls the appearance of a time gone bye, but also a fresh, new feel. The floors also appeared to be original, but beautifully restored as well. He didn't notice any cracks or slanting that would indicate structural issues.

"You can tell the town really went to a lot of work to keep the old style while updating the inside," Peter said. He couldn't wait to see what Chuck came up with. His hope was that these would be easy fixes so they wouldn't have to be leveled. "Are there any interesting stories associated with this building?"

"As a matter of fact," Chandler replied, "the post office was an essential part of the town during the Civil War. The women of the town would come here with the hopes of receiving a letter from their loved one fighting in the war. It was a great way for them to support each other while waiting for their men to return. And for some, it was where they received word that their loved one would not return, so the support of the other ladies in the community was crucial.

The post office was the source of news for the community. Since the branch was established prior to the Civil War and both Union and Confederate supporters resided in the area, the war and news about local soldiers were most likely main topics of conversation. There were no telephones or internet back then, of course. It's so hard to imagine what they went through, and the days, weeks, or even months they waited to hear any news."

"It definitely makes you rethink everything we take for granted today," he replied. "I'm so glad I have such a lovely tour guide to tell me about the rich history in Hope Springs." Once again, Peter swore he saw Chandler blushing. He wondered if anyone had ever paid her a compliment. That was their loss and his gain.

Chandler could feel her cheeks betraying her by heating up, not for the first time in the past few hours. Men had paid her compliments before, but her body had never reacted this way. She knew Peter was different from the men she had dated, but she didn't think he was *that* different. "So, are you ready to go get Rosie and have lunch?" she asked, looking at her watch.

"Ready when you are," Peter answered. He opened the door for her to lead the way.

On the block between the post office and the diner, they passed the Everything's New Again Boutique consignment shop and Jack Smith's CPA firm. Chandler explained that these buildings were used as the Apothecary Shop/Civil War Hospital. "Hillary and Jack Smith own both buildings now. He is the local town CPA and she runs the consignment shop. When they purchased the property ten years ago, it had been severely neglected. Rather than tear the buildings down, they worked to restore them. I'd love to see my building get the same treatment, but it's one of the hazards of having a landlord instead of owning the property yourself," she broke off in a sigh.

"It looks from the outside like they have done a great job," Peter said. He wasn't sure why they were on the list to be demolished given their excellent condition. He was going to have to ask Cassia that question.

As they were walking on toward Rosie's Quilting Emporium, they noticed the mayor coming out of the Hilltop Restaurant across the street, with a group of people Chandler didn't recognize.

"I guess the mayor is courting a new round of developers," she said.

Peter immediately recognized them as some of his staff, but asked, "How do you know they are developers?"

"Andrea said that the mayor eats at the diner every day unless he is courting 'important' people. Then he takes them to the more upscale Hilltop Restaurant."

"Interesting," replied Peter. He couldn't recall them having a meeting scheduled with the mayor today. Another thing he was going to have to check on.

They walked into Rosie's just after 1:00 p.m. "Wonderful, you're here," Rosie said with a smile. "I'm starving."

"Then allow me to take you two lovely ladies to lunch," Peter said.

Rosie turned to MaryAnn. "Will you be okay here, for a while?" she asked.

"I'll be just fine," MaryAnn said. Waving her hand toward the door, she added "You go have lunch and don't worry about a thing."

"Alright then," Rosie said to Peter and Chandler, "let's go."

119

Peter held the door for Rosie and Chandler to walk into the warm afternoon sunshine. "Lead the way, ladies," he said.

Chapter 19

The Hope Springs Diner was an eclectic mix of old and new. The gleaming hardwood floors appeared to be original, much like those Peter had seen in the other establishments they had visited. There was a row of high-backed booths along one long wall, opposite a counter with stools. Behind the counter was an old-fashioned soda fountain, as well as shelves housing glass and dinnerware. The kitchen was toward the back.

In the middle of the room, patrons could dine at a mix of square and rectangular wooden tables. Peter noticed no two chairs were the same. "This place is awesome!" he exclaimed, looking around. "I love the décor."

"Andrea has done a great job of mixing many different styles to create a warm, welcoming ambience," Rosie said. "She's collected photographs and memorabilia highlighting years of town history and displayed them around for everyone to enjoy."

Once they were seated at a table in the center of the room and had ordered sweet tea for the table, Rosie asked, "So, Peter, have you learned all about the history of our town?"

"Chandler is certainly a wealth of knowledge," he said. "And I've learned you have a few ghosts roaming around as well."

"Oh, so Mabel told you about our lovebirds by the lake, I take it?" Rosie asked before taking a sip of her tea.

"Quite the story," he said. "Did you happen to know the illustrious threesome?"

"Actually, I did," Rosie said.

The waitress came to take their orders. Rosie and Chandler both ordered a Cobb salad, and Peter ordered the special of the day, a hot roast beef sandwich with mashed potatoes. "So the story is true?" he asked, curious.

"Well, the story of the murder and her committing suicide is true," answered Rosie. "As for the ghosts of the lovebirds by the lake, I have no firsthand knowledge of this. However, your mother did come home one night claiming she'd seen them. So maybe there is some truth to that one."

"That's so cool," Peter said. "What about the story of the ghosts of the men who had the shootout at the courthouse?"

"You'll have to talk to your Uncle Robert about that one. He and his buddies were up to no good one summer night and claim they were chased out of the field by a band of outlaws from the 1800s. Near as we can figure, it was either a group of re-enactors playing tricks on unsuspecting high school kids, or.....," Rosie let them think about what the other option was. "All I know is that your uncle and his friends had the wits scared out of them that night. They never went back to that field again," she finished, laughing.

"This town is not the sleepy little town I thought it was," Peter murmured as their orders arrived. He took a bite of roast beef commenting, "Delicious. I hope after eating all this, I'll still have room for the famous chocolate cream pie I've heard about."

Chandler laughed, "I'm sure you'll find a little space somewhere." She didn't think Peter would have any trouble finishing everything. She, on the other hand, had to watch what she ate.

"So, Chandler, where else are you taking Peter?" Rosie asked.

"We've pretty much hit the highlights on Main Street," Chandler said. "I was thinking of showing him the Cotton Mill. It's such a cool building," she said turning toward Peter, "and was once the mainstay for the town."

The door to the diner opened and in walked Myrtle and her posse. "Well, hello there!" Myrtle exclaimed. "I didn't think we would see you again today, Peter."

Chandler almost choked on her salad knowing she had practically followed them all over town by way of her little spies. True to form, Mabel had a guilty look on her face.

"Really?" Peter asked. "Because I'm pretty sure we saw at least one of you today who suggested we come here for lunch." He noticed the guilty look on her face.

Now Chandler had to stifle a laugh. Myrtle had finally met her match! Peter actually called her out on something.

"You know, Mr. Frederick," Myrtle went back to calling him by his surname, "it is not nice to disrespect your elders."

"Now, Myrtle, I mean no disrespect," he said, smiling. "It's been a pleasure seeing your beautiful faces all over town."

Chandler took this opportunity to really look at Myrtle's current choice of apparel. She had dangly, hot pink, ball earrings hanging from her ears, swinging back and forth on the small chain every time she moved her head. These coordinated nicely with the hot pink knit top and mint green double knit slacks she wore.

Chandler couldn't help but notice the matching mint green sandals and handbag completing the ensemble.

Myrtle just smiled. "Peter you really are a charmer, aren't you?" she commented, wagging her finger in his direction.

Rosie saved him from answering by asking, "So ladies, are you having a late lunch, or was there another reason you are interrupting ours?"

"We are here to have lunch, of course," said Myrtle dramatically. "The mayor was over at the Hilltop courting another group, and besides, the food here is so much better."

"Do you know which group it was?" asked Rosie.

"I think these people are connected to the blonde we saw him with last week. I thought I overheard them mention something about a meeting he had with her and that she would be looking to come back sometime next week," said Fran. "I sure wish I knew what the mayor was up to."

Peter listened intently to what was being said, while finishing off his lunch. He would definitely be having a conversation with his staff when he returned to the office in the morning. He felt like he was being lied to by his own employees and he didn't like it one bit.

"Well," said Fran, "we'll let you get back to your lunch and we'll go order ours. We'll see you tonight, Chandler?" she asked.

Chandler smiled when yet again they wanted to make sure she was at the Thursday night get together. "Yes, I think we are going to finish the quilt tonight, and I don't want to miss the joy of taking it off the frame."

The ladies said their goodbyes just as the waitress came to clear the lunch dishes and take their dessert order. Chandler just stuck to a cup of coffee, but Peter ordered the famous chocolate cream pie. Rosie abstained, saying she knew there would be a lot of goodies to eat later.

"So, back to the Cotton Mill," said Peter, "I'd love to see it." He was curious about the development potential.

"Chandler will take you after lunch," said Rosie. "I'll need to get back to the store and make sure everything is quiet so I can get my rest this afternoon."

"Are you feeling okay, Grandmother?" Peter asked. He hated the thought of her being ill, especially when they were just reconnecting. To look at her, you would think she was ten years younger.

Rosie patted his hand. "Yes dear, everything is fine. I just have a habit of overdoing it a little and need to recharge in the afternoon. Nothing serious."

Peter's slice of pie arrived and he proclaimed that his eyes may have been bigger than his stomach. "Wow! Chandler would you care to help me eat this?"

"You are all on your own on this one, my friend," Chandler replied, smiling. "I take in way too many sweets as it is, working in the bakery. Don't worry, we can walk to the Cotton Mill to help you burn the calories," she teased.

Once dessert was finished and the bill paid by Peter, they walked Rosie back to her shop. Peter proclaimed that he would weigh considerably more if he ate at the diner every day, but that the pounds definitely would be worth it.

Chapter 20

As Peter and Chandler walked back down Main Street toward Spring Street, which would take them to the mill, Peter took the opportunity to really look around. This section of town, starting with Hope Springs Mercantile three blocks back, next to Rosie's, was the heart of the town. For the most part the buildings had all retained the charm and character with which they were built. Really, with the exception of the bakery building, they had been preserved on the outside pretty well. He could tell that everyone who had a business here cared about not only their business, but the surrounding ones as well. This was certainly the definition of a community. He wasn't sure if he wanted to be the one to change that.

They turned left onto Spring Street next to the post office and headed into a residential area. He remembered from his childhood visit that this was where the mill workers lived. Most of the homes were small, one-story cottages, but he could see that many were being refurbished. Even this section seemed to be going through revitalization. "I see a lot of these homes are being restored," he said.

"Oh, yes," Chandler said, smiling. "Small families and couples are moving in and restoring a lot of them. It's so nice to see they aren't just tearing them down and building bigger homes in their place. The larger homes are on the other side of Main Street."

As they kept walking, Peter remarked about the interesting green house with the fuchsia door. For some reason Chandler wasn't ready to reveal that this was her home, but she was very curious as to his impression. "What do you think about the paint job?" she asked.

"It looks so inviting and I love the colors," he said, which surprised her. "I remember seeing these houses when I visited with my parents so long ago, but never went in one," he remarked. "I always thought they looked homey." Definitely not like the large home on the water he'd grown up in.

"Macy, whom you met the other night, is renting that one over there," Chandler said, pointing to the one across the street. "She'd really love to be able to own one in the future, though. She wants to be able to put her own personal touches on it."

They continued walking toward the vacant Cotton Mill. As they to the came end of Spring Street, the mill stood before them. The red brick on the outside of the two-story building was in terrific shape for something built in 1900. Peter could already visualize the building being turned into apartments, or even condos if the market dictated.

"What is the history of the Cotton Mill?" he asked as they walked up to the property.

"The Cotton Mill was built in 1900 by a group of local residents who wanted to preserve the cotton growing industry in the area. As the founders intended, the mill became and remained a mainstay in the local economy," Chandler explained. "It was very profitable with the exception of losses during the Great Depression. The mill workers lived in the surrounding cottages, provided by the company. The mercantile was the general store, even back then."

"When did the mill close?" Peter asked as he peered into the windows on the first floor, noting structurally it seemed pretty sound.

"About 1980," Chandler said. "As with many small mills in the area, business moved on to larger manufacturing plants."

"For a structure that has stood vacant for so long, it looks to be in great condition," Peter said. "I'm surprised there isn't really any vandalism."

"Oh, that's because the town takes great pride in the mill and has been making sure there is no mischief," Chandler explained. "Of course, the idea of a ghost walking around is a pretty good deterrent as well," she said, smiling.

"Okay, what's the ghost story here?" he asked, with skepticism.

"Remember the man who was thrown in the thrashing machine?" she asked.

"Yes, but I thought he and the broken-hearted woman he was having an affair with have been spotted down by the lake?" he remembered.

"Yes, that's true," said Chandler, "but supposedly you can hear his screams in the building from when he was being thrown into the machine. I haven't heard them, but the thought of it seems to be keeping the juvenile delinquents away."

"Hopefully that wouldn't keep potential investors away if this property is developed," Peter commented.

"What kind of investors and development?" asked Chandler warily. "The property is owned by the Town of Hope Springs." She hoped he wasn't talking about tearing the building down.

"This property would be ideal for apartments or condos and could have great income potential for the town as well. It looks to be structurally sound and could easily be subdivided and reconfigured," Peter explained.

"That's an interesting idea," replied Chandler. "Is this the kind of development your company does?" She was beginning to think she could trust Peter to keep the integrity of the town intact, unlike some of the other developers she had seen around town.

"As a matter of fact, yes," Peter said. "I would definitely be interested if the town is. I'll have to think about it and see how best to proceed."

"Well," said Chandler looking at her watch, "I hate to end our tour, but I need to get back to the bakery." They started walking back toward town.

Peter took notice of more of the homes being restored and thought the idea of redeveloping the Cotton Mill held more and more appeal. "Thank you so much for sharing your historical knowledge of the town with me. I had no idea about the ghosts and other interesting facts about this sleepy little town."

"My pleasure," said Chandler, smiling. "For a small town, it really does have a lot going on," she said proudly.

As they returned to the bakery, Chandler remarked that she was looking forward to seeing his engineer, Chuck, on Saturday. "I hope we can come to an arrangement. I will make whatever size cake he needs in order to not have to pay for the work out of pocket."

"I'm sure it will work out just fine. Here's my business card with my cell number," he said, handing her a card he retrieved from his wallet. "Let me know what he says."

"Okay," she said, taking the card from him.

Peter got this sly grin on his face. "You know," he began, "I have baseball tickets for Saturday evening, and I happen to remember you saying you like the Crusaders." He waited for it to sink in that he remembered meeting her in the city.

"How do you," she stopped mid-sentence. "How long have you known that we've met before?" she asked with an incredulous look on her face.

"Since that first night at Rosie's when she mentioned you owned the bakery. When I first saw you, I thought you looked familiar, but that was the giveaway. When did you remember?" he asked.

"That same night," she said, smiling.

"Well, you were doing a very good job of trying to ignore me," he teased.

"You've seen the ladies around here. If I had let on that I'd met you before, they would have pounced. As it is now, they won't leave me alone. I know I'm going to be grilled again tonight about what we did today," she said. Then she looked around and smiled conspiratorially. "I'm sure the spies are out watching us right now."

"You're pretty paranoid, aren't you," he laughed. "Maybe we should just continue our conversation on Saturday evening at the Crusaders game where no one will know us?"

She smiled. "I'd like that."

"Great," he said, clapping his hands. "Would you like to come to my place before the game and we can go from there?"

"Sounds great," she replied. She hadn't been to a game in a while, but was really looking forward to going.

"I'll call you tomorrow with the details," he said. "Text when you're free tomorrow and I'll give you a call. That way I'll also have your cell number."

"Good idea," Chandler smiled, feeling silly for not offering her number sooner. "That would be helpful."

By now they had reached Peter's car. As Chandler watched him get into his car and drive away, she realized she was looking forward to a Saturday night for the first time in a long time. When she walked into the bakery, both Gretchen and Luann were smiling. "What?" she asked.

"Oh, nothing," answered Gretchen. "I just haven't seen a smile on your face that big in, well, ever."

"Oh, now, let's get back to work. I want to have everything done early for the Saturday cake deliveries so we can get out of here on time Saturday."

"Why?" asked Luann, smiling. "Do you have a date?" she teased.

Chandler just smiled and got to work.

Chapter 21

The Thursday night meeting of the Advice Quilting Bee was quite eventful. After a yummy dinner of baked spaghetti, salad, bread, and assorted desserts, the ladies got down to the business of finishing the quilt.

Chandler knew she was probably going to be bombarded with questions about her day with Peter. She had spent a lot of her afternoon thinking back over their tour and was surprised to find that she was more than a little giddy at the prospect of seeing him on Saturday.

"Business at the bakery is so busy right now," Chandler said, in an effort to hopefully give the impression that she was going to be too swamped to have a social life for the next few days. "It's graduation weekend, and it seems every kid in Hope Springs needs a cake. Not that I'm complaining, of course."

Myrtle wasn't fooled in the least. "Oh, you think you'll be really busy *all* weekend," she said. "You have nothing else going on?"

Chandler looked at her. "I do have to meet with a structural engineer on Saturday, but until then, Gretchen, Luann, and I will be busy decorating cakes. We'll probably be at the shop well into the night on Friday night, because we also have to have baked goods ready for the cases on Saturday morning. Based on how many sweet rolls and donuts we sell, I don't think anyone has breakfast at home on Saturdays!"

Rosie looked up from her stitching. "Why do you need a structural engineer?"

"I don't know if you've noticed, but when you walk in front of one of the display cases, the floor sags. The landlord won't do anything about it and I'm worried for the safety of my customers," Chandler replied.

"That could cost a lot, don't you think?" asked Rosie.

"Fortunately, the engineer's daughter is getting married and needs a wedding cake. We're going to see if we can work out a bartering deal," Chandler said.

"That's a great idea," said Rosie. "It was so nice to have lunch with you and Peter today, dear. How was the rest of your tour? Did he like the Cotton Mill?"

Choosing to skip the first part of Rosie's statement, Chandler focused on the question about the mill. "Yes, he actually thought he could see some development potential in the building."

This perked up the ears of the rest of the group. "What kind of development potential?" asked Fran. "He said he wasn't in with the rest of the developers around town."

"He was thinking along the lines of apartments or condos," answered Chandler. "I told him the town owns the property, and he thought it could be a great income earner for Hope Springs."

"That's interesting," said MaryAnn. "It could also bring in potential customers to all our businesses."

"Would Peter be in charge of the project?" asked Rosie, finishing the feathering pattern she had been working on.

"That would be my guess," Chandler answered.

"Hopefully potential buyers don't find out the place is haunted. I'm not sure if I would want to live there," said Andrea.

Myrtle looked up from the square she was working on. "Oh, there's no truth to that old rumor. I honestly don't know why everyone is so worked up over these supposed ghosts anyway. I've lived here all my life and have never once had an encounter."

Fran couldn't let that one get away. "Myrtle, the way you dress you would scare all ghosts within twenty-five feet of you. They don't like bright colors!"

Myrtle gave Fran a look that shot daggers and went back to her quilting.

"Myrtle, are you feeling okay?" asked Macy, who was feverishly trying to complete the work in front of her. She wasn't as quick as the other ladies.

"Why do you ask?" snapped Myrtle.

"Well, normally you would have some kind of comeback for Fran," MaryAnn answered for Macy. Myrtle seemed to be in one of her moods, and MaryAnn didn't want her to take it out on poor Macy. She could see Macy was having enough trouble with her stitching as it was.

"Maybe Myrtle is just tired," replied Chandler, smiling. "She did have a very busy day today."

"Why would you say that, Chandler?" asked Myrtle, in her not so innocent tone.

"Oh, I don't know. Maybe because every time I turned around today, there you were."

"No ma'am," Myrtle replied defensively, "I wasn't at the visitor's center."

"Now, how did you know I was there today, Myrtle?" asked Chandler with a smile on her face, knowing full well the answer to that question.

"Oh, Myrtle," said Fran, shaking her head. "I think you should have quit while you were ahead."

"How did you know Chandler was at the visitor's center if you weren't there today?" asked Macy.

"You know, Macy," replied Myrtle. "Have you ever heard the expression 'young people should be seen and not heard'?"

"I believe the expression is 'children should be seen and not heard'," said Macy, defiantly, "and I'm not a child." She stifled the urge to stick her tongue out at Myrtle.

"So, answer the question, Myrtle," Andrea pressed. "How did you know Chandler was at the visitor's center if you, yourself, weren't there?"

Since Myrtle didn't seem to be in the mood to answer, Chandler informed the group that one of her spies, Mabel, was working there and saw her and Peter. They later saw Myrtle, Fran and Mabel at lunch at the diner. The guilty expression on Mabel's face had spoken volumes, and that she had told Fran and Myrtle about their visit to the visitor's center and the fact that they would be having lunch at the diner later.

"It's okay, Myrtle," said Chandler, getting up to give Myrtle a hug, "we still love you and your Little Old Lady Network."

"You know," said Myrtle, pouting, "I liked you a lot more when you didn't have a man in your life. You didn't seem to pick on me so much."

"I don't think I like us being referred to as the Little Old Lady Network," protested Fran. "I'm not little and I certainly don't think sixty is old. Haven't you heard that sixty is the new thirty?"

"It's just a term of endearment," answered Chandler. "And Myrtle, what makes you think I have a man in my life?"

"Oh, please!" exclaimed Myrtle. "We all know you spent the day with him today, and you are going to see a Crusaders game with him this weekend."

Chandler's jaw dropped. "How could you possibly know that? No one was around when he asked me before he left!"

Myrtle got a smug expression on her face. "Not all the people in my network are little old ladies." Letting that tidbit sink in, Myrtle turned to the group. "Let's get back to work so we can finish this darn quilt tonight."

Chandler couldn't believe it, but Myrtle actually got the last word in and she really did have spies everywhere!

Rosie surveyed the work going on with the quilt and proclaimed that it looked like they had about one more hour to go. "If we all stop talking about Chandler's love life and focus on what we are doing, we can get this done tonight."

"Yes, please focus on the quilt," said Chandler frustratingly. "It's much more important than my non-existent love life!"

The next hour flew by, but finally, as was always the tradition, Rosie and Myrtle finished the last two stitches. With a huge cheer from everyone, it was proclaimed that the quilt was completed!

The final stage of removing the stitching line markings and binding the quilt would be completed by MaryAnn, and then the quilt could go to the church bazaar a week from Saturday.

"What's our next project?" asked Candy.

"We're almost done piecing a red, white, and blue, full-size, star quilt. It's for Katrina Smith, who has been convalescing at the VA hospital. She was injured by an IED in Afghanistan and is finally coming home," said Myrtle.

"That's wonderful," said Hillary. "God bless her for her service to our country."

Looking at the clock, Rosie said, "Thank you all so much for your hard work. We'll have the next quilt loaded for us to begin next week. Everyone go home and get some rest."

They all walked out feeling a tremendous sense of accomplishment at completing another quilt.

Chapter 22

"Pat, can you please get Lance Clark on the phone!" Peter yelled as he entered the office the next morning.

Pat could tell he wasn't in the best possible mood. "Sure thing," she said, bringing him a cup of coffee. "How about if you calm down before you talk to him?"

Peter looked up from the messages he was going through. "Did you know there was a meeting for scheduled yesterday with the mayor of Hope Springs?"

"No, but that may be why Lance was trying to get ahold of you yesterday, and said you weren't returning his calls," Pat replied, pointing to the stack of messages he was going through.

"Oh, well, get him on the phone," Peter growled.

The fact that Cassia knew he was going to Hope Springs yesterday and didn't tell him that Lance was going to be there really bothered him. He didn't like the thought of her going behind his back. Once he talked to Lance, he was going to have to see what she was up to.

Pat buzzed his phone intercom to tell him Lance was on Line 1. "Lance, do you mind explaining why I wasn't told of a meeting with the mayor of Hope Springs?" Peter asked his employee.

"Hey, boss," said Lance. "Cassia set the whole thing up a couple of days ago and told me you were on board. I had a couple of questions, but you didn't return my calls yesterday."

Well, that was an utter lie. He was fuming now, but said, "Why didn't you call my cell phone when you couldn't reach me here?" His employees all had his cell number and were told to use it when they needed to reach him.

"Cassia said you'd be in the office all day, and if you weren't, that you didn't want to be disturbed on your cell," Lance explained. "She made it sound like the two of you had some personal business to take care of, if you know what I mean."

"Lance, when did she tell you this?" Peter asked, hoping it wasn't after he had run into her the previous morning.

"About 9:00 yesterday morning," Lance answered. Before they'd run into each other. He didn't like the direction Cassia was going and would have to put a stop to it. Soon.

Peter decided to let the matter drop with Lance. He was just doing his job. The adage 'don't shoot the messenger' came to mind. "What questions did you need answered?" he asked, to change the subject.

"Well, the mayor is all for tearing down four or more buildings, but to be honest, I looked at them and it looks like the businesses are really thriving in them. I was wondering if we should be rethinking this project," Lance stated. "The longer I talked to the mayor, the more I got the impression he was more interested in the money potential and less in the town itself. He said, and I quote, 'Ms. Collins said we have the opportunity to make this deal very profitable for both of us.' I almost got the impression he thought Cassia was in charge of the whole thing, not you."

"Interesting," said Peter, getting angrier by the minute. Thank goodness Lance was a man of integrity.

"Boss, have you met with the mayor yet? It honestly seemed to me like he had no idea who you were," Lance said.

Peter had been trying to lay low until he could figure out a way to make this project work for everyone. "No, I haven't. I have family in Hope Springs, and I'm trying to see if so much destruction is necessary before I let them know I'm in charge of the revitalization project."

"If it were up to me, boss, I wouldn't demo anything. From what I could tell, the only building in need of major repair is the one housing the bakery. The rest look pretty darn good, considering their age," Lance offered up.

"I know that Chuck is going down there tomorrow to do some recon for me," Peter told him, "especially the bakery. I'd appreciate it if you could keep all this between us. I'm not too trusting of anyone else right now, and I don't want to mess this up. It means too much to my family."

"You bet," said Lance. "How do you want me to handle Cassia if she starts asking questions?" And they both knew she would.

Peter knew this one was going to be tough. He had too much at stake to let her take over. "Just play along with everything she is proposing, for now. I'll take care of the rest," he advised. "But please keep me in the loop."

"Okay," replied Lance. "If I notice anything fishy going on that I don't think you've approved, I'll let you know immediately."

"Thanks, Lance," answered Peter, "and please call my cell from now on." He didn't want to miss any more important calls.

"Sure thing," said Lance.

Peter hung up the phone and rubbed his hands over his face. He had to come up with a way to deal with Cassia, and soon. The tinny sound of his ringtone sang into the room, jolting him from his thoughts. He glanced down to the caller ID. *Speak of the devil,* he thought. Ordinarily, he would be inclined to ignore it, but not anymore. From now on, he needed to know what she was up to, constantly. "Hello," he said, putting the phone on speaker.

"Well, Peter Frederick, it's about time you answered your cell phone," Cassia replied. Just the sound of her voice annoyed him. "Lance told me he tried getting ahold of you all day yesterday and you never answered your phone."

Another lie, thought Peter. "It seems he was under the impression I would be in the office all day, so he kept calling here."

"Oh, really," Cassia said, innocently. "I wonder where he would get that impression. He called me yesterday and I told him you would be in Hope Springs."

"Since you brought it up, did you know Lance had a meeting with the mayor of Hope Springs yesterday?" Peter asked.

"No, I didn't," Cassia lied. "I told him I would be meeting with the mayor sometime next week. I had no idea he was going there yesterday."

"Interesting," said Peter. "And when again do you have that meeting scheduled with the mayor?"

"Oh, well, we haven't set an actual day and time," Cassia told him. "I figured you and I would get together to finalize the revitalization proposal first. Are you free on Monday?"

"Yes, be in my office Monday morning at 9:00 with your proposal," Peter said forcefully. "Remember, Cassia, I have to give my final approval on anything we move forward with. Don't forget that."

"Okay, Peter," Cassia answered strangely. "I'll see you then."

Peter hung up the phone without saying goodbye and yelled for Pat to come in his office. "I'm meeting with Cassia on Monday morning, here, at 9:00 a.m. Please put it on my calendar. And call Lance and Chuck and have them meet me here at 8:00 a.m. that morning with all they have on the Hope Springs project."

"Okay," said Pat, "anything else?"

Peter thought for a minute. "Yes, would you please send a red, white, and blue carnation Crusaders themed arrangement to Chandler Bradford at Sweet Stuff Bakery? Have the card read, 'Looking forward to our evening together, Peter'.

Pat smiled. "Oh good, hopefully this means you've given up on finding someone in the city, and found a nice, small town girl."

Peter just smiled and told her to take care of it.

Chapter 23

Chandler woke up Saturday morning with a lot more energy than she should have had. She, Gretchen, and Luann had put in a marathon decorating and baking session on Friday that lasted into the wee hours of Saturday morning. They not only finished every cake order, but also prepped a lot of the Saturday morning baked goods to finish when they got in this morning. She looked at the clock and saw that it was just after seven.

Chandler went into the kitchen and started the single-cup brewer. She knew she was going to need lots of coffee to get through the day, but knowing that she was going to end her day with Peter made everything brighten. They had spoken briefly the day before and made plans for later. She would be driving to his place and then they would head to the ballpark. Chandler was also looking forward to eating ballpark staples for dinner. There was nothing else quite like a having a hot dog, fries, and a cold drink at the ballpark while watching her favorite team.

After her coffee was ready, Chandler showered and got dressed for the bakery. Luckily, she would have time once they closed to come back and change for the ballgame. She walked the couple of blocks to Main Street, which seemed to be busy for an early Saturday morning, until she remembered it was Graduation Day and lots of folks would be coming into town.

She got to the bakery a little before 8:00 a.m., and saw that both Gretchen and Luann were already hard at work. They each definitely deserved a bonus as soon as she could afford it!

"Good morning, ladies," Chandler said as she came in the front door. She relocked it, but knew there would soon be a line and they would probably have to open early. She didn't mind doing that on Saturday for folks just wanting a cup of coffee and a treat instead of a full breakfast at the diner.

"Hi," answered Luann. "I think we are just about ready if you'd like to check the cases. The register and coffee are all set."

"Can we keep Luann forever?" asked Gretchen, smiling. "She makes my job so much easier."

"I wish," Chandler answered, agreeing that Luann was a wonderful addition to her small staff. There was a knock at the door with someone holding a giant floral arrangement done in red, white, and blue. "What in the world?" exclaimed Chandler, going toward the door.

"Delivery for Ms. Chandler Bradford," said the young delivery boy, trying very hard not to drop the arrangement.

"I'll take it," said Chandler. She thought the arrangement might outweigh the poor kid. "Here," Chandler said, handing the boy a twenty dollar bill. "Thanks."

The kid looked like he'd never received a tip before. "Thank you!" he said, staring at the bill before stuffing it in his shirt pocket. "Have a great day," he told them before turning and walking out.

"Is that a Crusaders flag sticking out of there?" asked Gretchen, incredulously.

The scent of fresh flowers was a welcome change to the cinnamon and buttercream icing they'd been smelling for days. "Yes," answered Chandler, taking the card and opening it, not that she needed to read the card to know who sent it. She smiled and asked the girls to help her find a place for the flowers.

Luann suggested on top of one of the cases by the window. "That way everyone walking by can enjoy them."

"Great idea," Chandler agreed. "Open the doors and let's get this day started. I have one client meeting today, but the rest of the time I can help with the customers."

"Man your stations, ladies," Gretchen shouted. "It's about to get crazy in here."

True to form the day flew by. Chandler had a great meeting with Chuck and his daughter. Chuck thought the work on her flooring could be completed fairly quickly. Chandler worked up a cake estimate for his daughter and they both agreed they could barter for the labor. It seemed like she was going to be able to afford the repairs after all.

At about 3:00 p.m., Gretchen wiped frosting on her apron and proclaimed, "Ladies, I do believe its closing time!"

"Whew, I don't think it's ever been that busy," said Chandler, locking the front door.

Luann looked at the cases. "There's nothing left to give to the fire department. We're sold out."

"Oh, I have a tray in the back that I saved for them," smiled Gretchen. "We don't want to forget them, especially since tomorrow is Sunday and we're closed. I'll get it boxed up and drop it off on my way home. Chandler, I know you want to go change before you head to Peter's, so Luann and I can take care of closing. I'll do the night drop on my way to the fire station."

"Thanks so much," answered Chandler. "I don't know what I'd do without both of you!"

"Go on ahead," urged Luann, pushing Chandler toward the door. "We've got everything handled from here. I'll lock up after you."

"I think I'll leave the flowers where they are. They dress the place up a bit," Chandler said as she was going out the door.

Chandler made the short walk to her house and could barely contain her excitement as she got ready for what she hoped would be a really great evening. Dressed in jeans, a Crusaders t-shirt and tennis shoes, Chandler grabbed her purse and keys, put her sunglasses on her head, and headed out the door.

Chapter 24

Chandler programmed Peter's address into the GPS, turned on her favorite tunes, and backed out of her driveway. The GPS said it would take about an hour to get to his apartment and she hoped that factored in Saturday traffic.

Luckily, the GPS was accurate and she arrived at his building right on time. He had told her to go to the underground parking and he would let the attendant know she was his guest, this way she could avoid paying for parking. She took the elevator to the main floor, where she met Carl, the doorman.

"Good evening, may I help you?" asked Carl.

"Yes, my name is Chandler Bradford and I'm here to see…."

Carl interrupted, smiling, "Yes, Ms. Bradford, it's so nice to meet you. I've heard a lot about you."

"All good, I hope," Chandler replied with an answering smile.

"Most assuredly," said Carl. "Mr. Frederick told me to let him know as soon as you arrived. Please take the elevator to the fifteenth floor and I'll let him know you're on your way up."

"Okay, thank you," said Chandler, turning toward the bank of elevators. As Chandler got on the elevator, she couldn't help but think about how vastly different her life was from Peter's. She had a cottage with a fuchsia pink door and he had a doorman named Carl and lived on the fifteenth floor! As the elevator rose, her resolve started to go in the other direction. *Maybe he is out of my league,* she thought. But before she could push the down arrow button, the elevator stopped and the door opened and she was greeted with Peter's smiling face.

"Hello," he said, smiling.

Okay, maybe she wasn't so far out of her league. Chandler got off the elevator, and all she could do was laugh.

"What's so funny?" he asked, frowning. He was dressed in a Crusaders jersey, baseball cap, and jeans.

"Well, it looks like we shopped at the same gift shop! I bet you are even wearing Crusaders socks and underwear," Chandler said with a giggle.

Peter leaned in. "Now let's not spoil all my surprises," he whispered, smiling. "Are you?"

"A lady never reveals all her secrets," was her reply. She went on to thank him for the floral arrangement. "We put it on a display case in the front window so the whole town could enjoy it."

"Wonderful," he said. "I must say you look mighty fine in that t-shirt."

"Clearly, I'm not as intense as you, but I am a fan," she said waiving her hand up and down to emphasize his attire again.

"Come on, I'll show you my place before we go," he said. His condo was two doors from the elevator, on the right. Chandler was really interested to see where Peter lived. The hallway seemed more like an expensive hotel hallway, but she hoped his condo had more of his personality.

He opened the door and stepped aside for her to enter. As Chandler entered, the first thing to greet her was the view. The bank of floor-to-ceiling windows was magnificent, affording an unobstructed view of the city below. But looking around, Chandler didn't see one personal item displayed, not even pictures of family or friends. Compared to her own home, Peter's felt to her more like a hotel room. *No*, she thought, *a hotel room had more warmth.*

"Not quite as homey as Hope Springs, is it?" Peter asked, watching Chandler take it all in.

"The view is spectacular," Chandler dodged the question, "and, besides, you're a bachelor in the city. How homey should it be?"

Peter saw that she was clearly trying to make him feel better about the lack of color and warmth his place projected. "Unfortunately, I'm not much of a decorator, and this is what you get when you pay someone to take care of it for you. It's more like a magazine cover than a home. I'm guessing your place has more color," he said, smiling.

"You'd be surprised," laughed Chandler, knowing that he had already commented on the color of the exterior of her home without knowing it was hers.

Peter looked at his watch. "Let's head out to the ballpark. Jake gave me his parking pass along with the tickets, so we can park close. If we leave now, we'll have enough time to get something to eat and watch batting practice before the game."

"That sounds like a great idea," smiled Chandler, "and besides, I'm starving for ballpark food!"

Peter double-checked to make sure he had the tickets and held the door for Chandler to exit the condo. Once they got to the bank of elevators, he pushed the down arrow and stepped back in case anyone would be exiting. Unfortunately, Chandler hadn't done the

149

same, and before she knew it, the door opened and a shorter, blonde woman ran right into her.

"Oh!" exclaimed Cassia.

"Excuse me," said Chandler, trying not to lose her balance from the impact.

"Watch where you're going, lady," Cassia admonished. "It's customary to wait for the elevator to clear before entering."

"If I had seen you, I would have waited," Chandler answered. She took a closer look at Cassia, with the uncomfortable sensation that she had seen her before. "Have we met?" she asked.

Cassia looked at her as if to say, *you must be joking*, and coughed, "I highly doubt it." When Cassia saw who was behind the woman who ran into her, the look of shock was all over her face.

Peter could see the wheels turning in Cassia's brain. She did indeed remember seeing Chandler somewhere before, and would be wracking her brain to figure it out, too. He had to diffuse the situation, quickly. "Cassia, this is Chandler Bradford, and Chandler, this is Cassia Collins," he said, ushering Chandler into the elevator. Right as he was pushing the button for the door to close and send them to the lobby, he said, "It was nice to see you again, Cassia."

Cassia stood there looking at the closed elevator door. *Where have I seen that woman before and why was Peter in such a hurry to whisk her away?* What aggravated her even more was the fact that he had lied to her. He had said he was going to the game with Jake, and that was definitely not Jake! She pushed the elevator down button to call the next car, hoping she could catch them in the lobby.

"So, do you want to tell me what that was all about?" asked Chandler, as she and Peter were headed down to the lobby.

"Old flame," was all Peter said. The door to the lobby opened and he practically pushed her out. He looked over at Carl, who indicated that he tried to warn him, and then ushered Chandler to the parking garage and his car. He didn't want to take a chance that Cassia would reappear.

Once they were safely in the car, he turned to Chandler, "I'm so sorry for that," he apologized. "I hope you don't think I'm one of those guys who have girls all over town showing up out of nowhere. I had no idea she was coming, and frankly, I'm not sure why she did."

Lucky for him, Chandler wasn't the jealous type, but she did think she had seen Cassia before. "It's alright. Let's not let that little interruption ruin our night. I've been looking forward to the game all day," she said, smiling. It wasn't like Chandler hadn't dated anyone besides Peter ever in her life.

Peter started the car and drove them out into Saturday evening traffic toward the ballpark. He knew he'd have to answer to Cassia on Monday, but for now he could devote all his attention to Chandler.

Cassia burst out of the elevator, fuming. She stomped over to Carl and practically screamed, "Just who was that with Mr. Frederick?!"

Carl just smiled and said he was not allowed to divulge information about residents and their visitors.

Cassia gave another little scream, causing several residents and visitors to jump. She stomped out the door, just in time to see Peter's car leave the parking garage. *There is definitely something familiar about that woman,* she thought, *and I'm going to figure out what it is or die trying.*

"This has to be the best hot dog I've ever had," said Chandler, taking a bite of her hot dog after they had found their seats at the ballpark, "and washing it down with a cold beer makes it even better!"

"You are definitely not like most of the women I've dated," observed Peter.

"What do you mean?" asked Chandler, taking a couple of fries and dipping them in ketchup before popping them in her mouth.

"First of all, most of them wouldn't be caught dead at a baseball game," he said holding up his index finger. "Second," he said, holding up another finger, "none of them would be caught dead eating a hot dog with the works, fries loaded with sugary ketchup, and drinking an extra-large beer!"

"Well, if you expect me to apologize for it, you can forget it," answered Chandler, taking another bite of hot dog.

"Oh, heck no!" exclaimed Peter. "You are quite a refreshing change. I'd much rather be dressed like this at a ball game, than dressed in a tuxedo at another boring museum fundraiser."

"As handsome as I'm sure you are in a tux," said Chandler, "I think I prefer you dressed as you are now. So much more approachable."

"I seem to remember the first time we met, you were all dressed up for an art gallery opening, am I right?" asked Peter.

"Yes, I was," Chandler confirmed. Then she figured she might as well tell him about Victor. "I was dating Victor Confer, of the Confer Art Gallery."

"Oh, yeah?!" Peter had been to many art shows at the Confer Art Gallery, and Victor Confer didn't seem to be Chandler's type. "What happened? You were a bit frazzled when you came into Crandy's," he noted.

"Well, I had just learned that Victor had been using me to get really good, really free baked goods for his openings. According to his business partner, the two of them had been having a fling for about six months prior to that night," she said, taking a sip of her beer.

"Ouch," he said, "that must have hurt for her to say it like that."

"Him," Chandler corrected. She couldn't help but smile as Peter got awfully still and silent. "That's okay, I laughed when I realized it too. Apparently, I bat for the wrong team," she finished with a wink.

Peter threw back his head with laughter. "Well, his loss is definitely my gain." He picked up his drink and then clinked it to hers in a silent toast.

Chandler smiled. "Are you for real, Peter Frederick? I've never met any man, city or country, like you."

"I can prove to you I'm real," smiled Peter, and with that he leaned over and kissed her. "Real?"

"Oh, I hope so," Chandler said, dreamily.

"Great, now let's enjoy a wonderful night at the ballpark!" exclaimed Peter.

Chandler hoped this night, and this feeling, would never end.

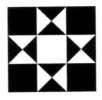

Chapter 25

Chandler woke up Sunday morning wondering if the previous night had been a dream. She and Peter had so much fun cheering the Crusaders on to victory. He'd invited her in for a drink after the game, but since it had gone to extra innings and hadn't been over until after midnight, she felt it best to head home. He'd insisted she call him when she got to Hope Springs so he'd know she made it home safely. Not since her grandmother had been alive had anyone cared whether she made it somewhere safely or not.

She looked at the clock and saw that if she got moving she could make it to church on time. The pastor would be honoring the high school graduates who were members of the church, and she knew a couple of them well. She got ready and headed out the door just in time to walk with Macy.

It was a warm, sunny morning, and Chandler was glad she'd worn a sleeveless dress and remembered to grab her sunglasses. "Good morning, Macy," Chandler said as Macy crossed the street.

"Good morning to you! I'm so glad we have a little time so you can tell me all about your date last night," Macy said, giving Chandler a hug and looping her arm through Chandler's for the stroll to the church. "Glad I decided to skip the jacket that I usually wear with this dress. I heard it's going to be a warm one today."

"I agree," Chandler said in answer to Macy's last statement. And in answer to the first, she smiled and sighed. "It was wonderful. I swear I have never met a man like Peter. I think I had totally misjudged him in the beginning. He was a perfect gentleman, and so down to earth."

"I'm so glad," Macy replied, happy for her best friend, "and I bet he's a great kisser."

"I'm not one to kiss and tell," Chandler said with a wink and a smile. They turned and began walking toward Main Street.

"When are you going to see him again?" asked Macy as they walked past the post office.

"Probably sometime this week. We haven't set another date," said Chandler. "But something strange happened when we were leaving his penthouse."

"Penthouse?" asked Macy, surprised.

"Yes," answered Chandler, "on the fifteenth floor overlooking the river."

"Okay, you can fill me in on the penthouse details later. What strange thing happened?" Macy asked, looking both ways before they crossed Main Street. They turned right and began walking the two blocks north to the church.

"The elevator door opened and this woman came out so quickly she practically ran me over," Chandler told her. "Peter introduced us and said her name was Cassia, before practically shoving me into the elevator. He later told me she was an old flame."

"What's strange about that?" Macy asked. She figured lots of people had old flames they were bound to run into on occasion.

"Well, why was she there, for one? And second, it was one of those things where I could have sworn I've seen her before," Chandler said, quizzically. "It's going to really bug me until I figure it out."

"Oh, I hate it when that happens," Macy agreed. "I usually wake up in the middle of the night remembering, and then I can't go back to sleep."

"I've had that happen, too," Chandler said, chuckling, as they arrived at the church. She removed her sunglasses as they walked in the front door.

"Do you suppose she lives in the building and was just coming home?" Macy asked when they were walking up the aisle toward their seats, trying to come up with an explanation.

"It's possible," whispered Chandler, before greeting Rosie, Myrtle, and Fran. Chandler knew that Myrtle would want to know all about last night, but she didn't want to talk about it in church.

They all took their seats as the service began. Chandler loved having this one hour a week where she could collect her thoughts and listen to the message from the pastor. He always seemed to have a sermon that spoke to her and this week was no different. His message, though likely intended for the high school students, was that God put people in our paths for a reason, and it was our job to figure out what that reason was. Do not question, but accept God's plan for us. *So, if God's plan is for Peter to be in my life, then who am I to question it?* thought Chandler, smiling. She would just relax and see where God took the relationship.

Once the service was over, Rosie invited Chandler for a cup of tea at her house. "Just you and me," Rosie said, smiling and patting Chandler's hand.

"I'd like that," answered Chandler quietly so others wouldn't overhear. Chandler knew Rosie was curious about her date with Peter and didn't want to have this conversation with the others around. They said their goodbyes to the group and walked to Rosie's.

Once they got to the porch, Rosie said, "Oh my, I didn't realize how warm it had gotten while we were in church. I think I'll go change out of this suit and into something a little cooler. While I'm doing that, would you mind getting a tray together with iced tea and cookies? I think it's too hot for anything but iced tea." Chandler had noticed that Rosie was dressed in a dark rose pantsuit. The white blouse under the jacket had a big bow around the neck. Since she was quite warm in her lavender floral sheath dress, she had wondered how Rosie could keep her jacket on in church.

"Please go and make yourself comfortable," answered Chandler. "I'll take care of everything else and meet you on the porch."

While Rosie went upstairs to change, Chandler went about getting everything on a pretty silver tray she found. Rosie already had a pitcher of sweet tea in the refrigerator, so she put that, along with two glasses filled with ice, on the tray. Chandler found a cookie jar on the counter containing sugar cookies from her bakery. She put them on a small plate and added that to the tray, along with a couple of napkins and plates for each of them.

Just as Chandler was carrying the tray out to the porch, Rosie came down the stairs dressed in a light blue, floral, sleeveless top and white capris. "I feel so much better," said Rosie. "I could have sworn it was supposed to be cool this morning. Here, let me get the door for you," she added, holding to door for Chandler to pass through.

Chandler put the tray on the table and poured them each a glass of tea. She put two cookies on each of their plates and handed a glass and plate to Rosie. After Chandler took a bite of her cookie, she proclaimed with a grin, "These are the best cookies in town!"

"Well," said Rosie, smiling, "I happen to know the baker really well. Perhaps she could give you the recipe."

"Perhaps," smiled Chandler. She looked around the wide veranda where Rosie grew a wide array of flowers that all smelled heavenly. "I may be good at baking, but I could never be as good as you at gardening, Rosie. This porch smells wonderful!"

"Thank you," Rosie accepted the compliment. "I'm glad you agreed to come, my dear," she continued. "I've been so excited to hear how your date with Peter went, but I didn't want to ask in front of the others."

"I appreciate that," answered Chandler, taking a sip of the chilled sweet tea. "We had a wonderful time. Peter is nothing like what I thought he was. I mean, no offense, but in the beginning I thought he came across as a little arrogant. He's really nothing like that at all, is he?" Chandler thought she was a good judge of character, but maybe she was wrong this time.

Rosie smiled. "Yes, Peter is very sure of himself in the business world, and he really does seem to be the type to thrive in the city. Deep down, though, I think there is a little bit of the country in him as well. You may just be the person to bring that to the surface."

"He was such a gentleman," Chandler told her. "He even asked me to call when I got home to make sure I made it safely."

"I'm happy to hear this, Chandler. I always wondered if he would grow up to be a caring person," Rosie said, pleased to hear this. "His parents were a little too self-absorbed for my liking."

"Rosie," started Chandler, "I'm not sure how far this is going to go, but I'm beginning to think I'd like the relationship to continue to grow." She had to admit this was the first time she actually wanted a relationship to continue. Even with Victor, she somehow knew he wasn't the one. "How did you know when Mr. Macintire was the one for you?"

"Well," Rosie said, putting her glass on the table, "as I've said before, Charles and I knew each other for a few years before we started dating. We were friends first, but as we continued seeing each other and talking about our life goals and where we wanted to be in life, I knew. I guess the bottom line for me was we had the same vision for our lives. It's hard to build a life together if you want different things."

Chandler took a bite of cookie and sip of tea so she could ponder what Rosie had said. "Well, I know I want to stay in Hope Springs and continue running my bakery. I'm not sure how that translates into a life with Peter if he wants to live in the city and continue running his company from there."

"I think those are the kinds of conversations you will need to have. A relationship cannot work unless both sides are willing to compromise," Rosie advised. "There's no need to rush, though. Let the relationship grow and see what happens."

"I'm so glad we were able to visit today, Rosie," said Chandler gratefully. "Other than Myrtle, you are the closest thing to a relative I have left. Bless Myrtle's heart, but I just can't trust her with this kind of conversation. It would be all over town in no time flat!"

"You are very special to us," said Rosie, knowing Chandler was right about Myrtle. "Myrtle just wants what's best for you, like we all do, and with a little luck, that will be my grandson," she declared with a huge smile.

Chandler smiled and finished her tea and the last bite of her cookie. "Well, I think I'd better head home," she said, getting up. "I have a house to clean and laundry to do. I know it's Sunday, but with working at the bakery six days a week, it's the only time I can get stuff done at home."

As they were getting up, Chandler asked, "May I carry this in for you?" indicating the tray and empty dishes.

"I don't think that'll be necessary," said Rosie, motioning toward the sidewalk. Myrtle was making her way over. Seeing the look on Chandler's face, Rosie said, "Don't worry, our conversation is just between us. Now you run along and I'll visit with Myrtle."

"Hello, Chandler," Myrtle shouted as Chandler was coming down the front steps and Myrtle was walking up the sidewalk. "What's your hurry?" she said a little annoyed that Chandler was leaving. The whole point of her coming to Rosie's was to grill Chandler on her date with Peter.

Chandler noticed Myrtle had also changed from a sedate, light green dress with matching sandals and handbag into an orange, flowery top and orange shorts outfit. She also noticed her interesting choice in footwear. "Myrtle, are you wearing flip flops?" Chandler asked by way of distraction.

"Yes," Myrtle answered. "The girl at the shoe store told me they were the most comfortable shoe I would ever wear. I believe she was right!" She held up one foot and wiggled her toes.

"Come on up, Myrtle," Rosie yelled from the porch. "Let's leave Chandler to go on with her busy day. I've got sweet tea and sugar cookies from the bakery."

"If I do say so myself, the cookies are delicious," smiled Chandler as she gave Myrtle a hug, waved to Rosie, and started down the sidewalk.

"Wait! I wanted to hear all about your date," yelled Myrtle, but Chandler just kept on walking.

"Now, Myrtle, leave the poor girl alone and get on up here and out of the sun," admonished Rosie. "It's not good for your skin."

Myrtle looked from Rosie to Chandler and back to Rosie. She decided she'd better do as Rosie said, this time.

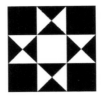

Chapter 26

Peter had spent Sunday with Jake at the afternoon game and had filled him in on everything. And, while the company wasn't nearly as cute as the previous night, he knew he could tell Jake anything and it would go no further.

"It sounds to me like Cassia wants your company and 'your company'," said Jake, using air quotes for emphasis with a waggle of his eyebrows.

"I know," said Peter, drinking his beer, "and I'm hoping she and Chandler didn't recognize each other in the elevator. I know Cassia has seen pictures from inside the bakery that her assistant took for the revitalization project, and I just hope Chandler wasn't in any of them." He also knew Cassia had been in Hope Springs enough times for her to stick out like a sore thumb. No one in Hope Springs dressed the way she did or drove a little convertible like she did.

"What are you going to do if either one of them figures it out?" asked Jake, knowing trying to keep two women from finding out about each other was a sticky problem to have.

"Pray," Peter had answered.

That was the thing. Peter didn't know what he was going to do. If Chandler found out he was in charge of the revitalization project before he had everything ready to take to the mayor, that would be it for their relationship. Plus, he knew for a fact that Cassia would think nothing of hurting Chandler, and ultimately his grandmother, by telling all before he was ready.

Peter woke up Monday morning, ready to do battle with Cassia. He got to the office at 7:30 a.m., ready to meet Chuck and Lance at 8:00 a.m. Peter asked Pat to bring them each coffee, and then closed the door. He didn't want to risk anyone overhearing this conversation.

"So, Chuck, why don't you start? What did you find out about the bakery building?" Peter asked, referring to the meeting Chuck had had with Chandler over the weekend. Chandler had told him they'd reached a barter for work, but he wanted to know the extent of the damage from an engineering perspective.

Chuck put the photographs of the structure in front of Peter. "As you can see, I think we can save the entire building by just shoring up two or three floor joists underneath. We could open up the crawl space and slide them in. It's really not as bad as it could be. The rest of the structure looks great."

"That's what Chandler thought she understood," said Peter, "and that you were able to barter for the work."

"Yep," answered Chuck. "She's going to make a wedding cake for my daughter and I'm going to fix the floor."

"Was it really equal?" asked Peter, knowing how much the construction work would cost, but having no idea what a wedding cake would cost.

"Well," said Chuck, "it was close, but I'm willing to call it even. We have the supplies in our extra inventory to do the work, so it really is just the labor. Besides, she has a booming bakery business and I'd hate to see that go away." Peter liked that he and Chuck were on the same page.

"Thanks, Chuck," said Peter. "You're a good man." Turning to Lance, he asked, "Show me again what Cassia has proposed to the mayor." He wanted to make sure the plans she showed him earlier were the same as what Lance showed the mayor.

Lance rolled out the drawings on the work table in Peter's office. "As I'm sure you know," he started, "she is proposing we level two blocks worth of buildings on each side of Main Street, including the library, visitor's center, and bakery. To be honest, I don't think it's necessary." Peter liked the sound of that.

"I agree," Chuck interjected. "My daughter and I looked at all those buildings, and aside from the bakery, they're all structurally sound, and the stories each one tells are so unique. Did you know there are ghosts in Hope Springs?" Chuck asked, clearly excited at the prospect of encountering one.

"Yes, so I've been told," Peter replied dryly, laughing inside but trying to downplay the possibility.

"Okay, let's say we don't level them. Do we have another way to revitalize the area?" Peter asked Lance. "Just what does the mayor hope to accomplish?" If there was some way around this, he was all for it.

"I know they want to bring in some office space and promote Hope Springs as a great destination for smaller companies looking to do business in a small town atmosphere," explained Lance. "The mayor thinks the tax revenue from these new companies would be great. From my opinion of him, it seemed like he would be getting the financial boost, not the town."

"So, the bottom line is that the mayor wants office space," Peter concluded. This was the first he was hearing of this. He was under the impression they were looking more at retail and housing space. Office space didn't necessarily need to be on Main Street.

"Is there any other property on Main Street that could be converted to office space?" asked Peter, looking at the drawings.

"That's a good question," answered Lance. Looking at the table, he pointed to the space near the war monument. "Right now this is a park. Unfortunately, it's pretty run down and really in need of some work. We may be able to convert that space."

"No," said Peter. "Let's leave the park. Maybe we can get it in the plans to fix that up as well." He figured that they could use that as a bargaining chip with the residents. His company would fix up the park while adding more to Main Street.

Chuck looked at the plans again. "What about this space behind the police station?" he asked, pointing to what looked to be vacant space. "This is a good, two-block area and there's already a parking lot one block over behind the mercantile."

"I like where you're going with this Chuck," Peter said, encouraged by this meeting. "Lance, do me a favor and draw up a set of plans and specs using any other available land that's not right on Main Street. Part of the charm of Hope Springs is driving down the historic Main Street, and I'd like to leave it that way."

"You bet," said Lance, rolling up the plans. "I can have it to you by the end of the week."

"Gentlemen, thanks for all your hard work," Peter told them, walking toward the door. "I'd appreciate it if this conversation goes no further than this office. If you have any questions, please call my cell, not Cassia." He opened the door and saw that Cassia wasn't in the outer office.

"Sure thing," they answered as they walked out the door.

Peter looked at the clock and saw that it was 8:45. He had a little time to regroup before Cassia came in. He picked up his cell phone and pushed the speed dial for Chandler. He hoped to catch her before the bakery opened. As he waited for her to answer, he realized he had never programmed any of his other dates into his speed dial. That thought made him smile.

"Hello there," Chandler answered, knowing it was Peter on the line. She finished drying her hands on the towel she had grabbed when her phone was ringing.

"Hi," he said. "I hoped I would catch you before you opened."

"Yep, you did," she said, smiling. "I have a few minutes. What's up?"

"I was wondering what your week is looking like? I'd love to see you again soon," he said as he looked out the window at the people on the street below. He couldn't help but notice what a sharp contrast the busy street was to the peaceful setting of Main Street in Hope Springs.

Chandler smiled, "I'm free Wednesday night. How about if you come here this time and I fix you dinner?" She couldn't wait to see Peter again.

"I'd love that," he answered, "but you'll need to give me your address."

Chandler started laughing. "You actually already know where I live."

Peter was confused. He didn't remember going to her house on any of their tours. "No, I don't think I've been there before."

"Do you remember the green house with the fuchsia door?" she asked, smiling.

"Really?" he asked incredulous. "Why didn't you tell me that was your house?"

"I wasn't ready to reveal that then," she explained, "not until I was really sure about you."

"So you're sure now?" He was happy to hear he had passed that test; however, he felt guilty because he knew he hadn't been completely honest with her about his part in the revitalization project.

"Yes, definitely," Chandler smiled. "How about 6:30 Wednesday evening?"

"Wednesday, 6:30," he repeated. "Can I bring anything?"

"No," she answered, "I'll take care of everything. See you then."

Peter smiled. "Can't wait." He hung up in a much better mood.

A moment later, Pat announced that Cassia had arrived for their 9:00 a.m. appointment. And there went Peter's good mood. He told Pat to send her in, then stood up and walked toward the door.

"Peter, just who was that I saw you with at your place on Saturday?" Cassia asked by way of greeting. He noticed she was dressed in a short, teal blue skirt with a white blouse and teal jacket left unbuttoned. Her four-inch white heels made her appear taller than she really was.

"Just a friend," he answered matter-of-factly. "Do you have the revitalization proposal?" He didn't want to talk to her about Chandler.

"Well, yes," Cassia said, somewhat irritated, "right here." She rolled out the plans and handed him the written proposal. "See. Like I've explained before, we're planning on leveling these blocks," she said, pointing to the ones in question. "And the mayor would like us to build two, four-story office buildings in their place."

"And you're sure the mayor really doesn't care about the historical value of these structures?" he asked, to see if she really knew the answer to that question. "From what my grandmother and her friends have said, there is a lot of history there." He wasn't about to tell her about his tours with Chandler.

"Um, well," she stammered, "I'm not familiar with the history, however, the mayor would be, and he still wants them demolished. I guess the tax revenue from offices outweigh history, in his mind," she answered with a shrug of her shoulders.

This took Peter a bit by surprise since she was the one who had originally told him about the historical buildings. He wondered if Cassia was getting conflicting information from the mayor, or just having trouble keeping her lies straight.
"Have you scheduled your meeting with the mayor yet?" Peter asked, still looking down at the plans set before him.

"No, but I will as soon as you approve these plans," she answered, somewhat annoyed. "So, what do you say? Should we go ahead with this or have I wasted my time with this project? Because I, I mean we, plan to make a lot of money with this deal."

This last statement really alarmed Peter. "I'm not quite ready to give the approval yet. Do you have all the numbers so I can review them? I want to make sure this is really going to be profitable for *my* company," he said. He wanted to make it clear that any profits would be his, and potentially theirs if he was generous, and not *hers* alone.

"Well," she said with a huff, "I really don't understand why you need to look at them again, but I can get them for you in a day or so." She moved closer so they were almost touching, and said, "If I didn't know any better, Peter, I'd think you don't trust me."

Peter backed up a step, putting some space between them. "I'm just making sure everything is the way I want it. Why don't you set up a meeting with the mayor for a week from Friday for both of us to present the proposal?" He now knew the man had no idea who he was, and he needed to remedy that. Plus, by then he'd have his own proposal ready to present. "That will give me enough time to review the numbers again."

"I don't think it's necessary for you to attend," she started, but after seeing the stern look on his face, she dejectedly continued, "but, I'll let you know what time." She gave him what he was sure she thought was her sexy pouty face, and sauntered out the door.

Pat came in with a cup of coffee. "Do you want it straight or should I add something alcoholic?" Her disdain for Cassie was evident.

Peter dropped into his desk chair and rubbed his temples. "It's too early for that unfortunately, but if you have some aspirin that would be great. Also, if I have anything on my calendar after 4:00 on Wednesday afternoon, please cancel."

Pat smiled, "I'll get the aspirin and clear your schedule. Anything else?"

"No, that'll be all," he answered. Why was a five-minute meeting with Cassia so exhausting? He rubbed his temples and got to work.

Chapter 27

"You might have dodged me at church yesterday, Chandler, but I'm here to find out how your date with Peter went, and I'm not leaving until you tell me everything!" Myrtle had come bounding into the bakery, almost running into old Mr. Simpson in the process. Chandler looked up from decorating a cake to catch the near-miss with a shake of her head.

"Hello, Myrtle," replied Chandler. "As you can see, I'm a little busy here." She knew she couldn't dodge Myrtle forever, so she offered an alternative to having the conversation in the bakery. "Let's get together for lunch in an hour at the park and I'll tell you all about it."

Myrtle straightened her top over her mid-section, not really expecting Chandler to agree to talking so quickly. She was ready with a whole list of reasons why Chandler should tell her everything. "Okay," she replied instead, "I'll pick us up a couple of sandwiches and meet you there."

"That sounds like a great idea," Chandler said, smiling. "One of Andrea's chicken salad sandwiches would be wonderful!"

"I'll take care of it and meet you there," Myrtle told her, seemingly satisfied she'd be getting the scoop soon.

Chandler watched Myrtle walk out and then got back to work. She was decorating a cake for one of the members of the garden club who was turning seventy, and the customer hosting her party had requested a cake resembling a basket of flowers. The basket weaving technique took a long time and a steady hand, but the resulting look was spectacular when done right.

Chandler loved working on these kinds of cakes. She could immerse herself in her work and just let her mind wander. So much had happened over the past few weeks. If someone had told her three weeks earlier she would be dating another guy from the city, who was Rosie's grandson to boot, she'd have thought they were crazy.

But Peter was so different from Victor. If she hadn't known better, she would have sworn he'd grown up in Hope Springs. Even when she'd met him at his condo, he didn't seem like someone from the city. The décor of the place didn't fit the man she knew. He told her he had paid someone to decorate his place, and she could see they made no effort to get to know him or his personality.

Chandler was so excited to have him over to her place on Wednesday night. She wanted to come up with a menu that was small town charm. He had mentioned when they were at the diner, that he loved roast beef and mashed potatoes. Maybe she'd do a pork roast, mashed potatoes, green beans, and applesauce. It couldn't get much more small-town than that! She'd get an apple pie from the diner, too, just to send it over the top. Yes, she could bake one, but honestly Andrea's pie crust was much better. Chandler had no qualms sending customers requesting pies, to Andrea.

Chandler put the finishing touches on the basket portion and put the cake in the cooler. She'd finish the flowers and lettering later before her client came to pick it up. Looking up at the clock, she saw that it was almost time to meet Myrtle. "Gretchen, I'm going to head over to the park to have lunch with Myrtle," Chandler said, taking off her apron. She looked down at the icing

171

covered cloth and was glad she had put it on. She didn't always remember to do that.

"Okay," answered Gretchen, working on a cake of her own. "Luann and I can hold down the fort while you're gone."

Chandler went out the door, turned right, and walked the two blocks to the park. As she entered, she noticed someone unfamiliar was taking pictures of the area. Since there weren't any children there, she chose not to ask him what he was up to. A lot of parents let their 'tweens come to the park alone since it was a small town, but she was sure they still wouldn't want a stranger taking their kids' pictures.

Chandler chose a picnic table for her and Myrtle to have their lunch, and watched as the man snapped a few more pictures and then left. She looked around and saw Myrtle coming and waved her over.

"Who was that guy?" Myrtle asked, looking back at the man. She knew pretty much everyone in town, and this guy was new.

"I don't know. He was taking pictures of the park. Since there weren't any children present, I figured he wasn't a weirdo," Chandler said. "But since you've seen him, maybe you and your posse can keep an eye out for him," she added, smiling.

"Very funny," snapped Myrtle. "We do not spy, we are just very observant." Myrtle handed Chandler her lunch. Andrea always packed lunches in little boxes, complete with a drink, chips, cookies, and napkins.

"Thanks, I'm starved," Chandler said, opening her lunch. "Even though I'm around food all morning, I try very hard not to eat any of it."

"Okay, so tell me about Peter," said Myrtle, before she took a bite of her sandwich.

"Well, we had a very nice time." Chandler took a bite of her sandwich and sip of her drink.

"Oh no, you don't," Myrtle shook her finger at Chandler, knowing getting information out of Chandler was like pulling teeth. "You're not going to get away with 'we had a very nice time'. I want details."

"Okay, okay. I met him at his place and then he drove us to Crusaders Stadium for the game. We had hot dogs and beer and cheered the home team to victory. The game went into extra innings, so we decided not to go out for drinks after." Chandler stopped to take another bite of her sandwich and wash it down with her soda. "He drove us back to his place so I could get my car, and then I drove home. He asked that I call him when I got home, and I did." She popped a chip in her mouth and smiled.

"That was a very nice explanation of your itinerary," Myrtle admonished. "Now, did he kiss you?"

"Myrtle, I'm not going to answer that!" There were just some things Chandler wanted to keep private. She was also not about to tell Myrtle he was coming for dinner on Wednesday night, but she figured that secret would be out as soon as his car hit the town limits.

"Fine," said Myrtle. "I will just assume that he did and that it was wonderful. Are you going to see him again soon?"

Chandler figured Myrtle might just be a mind reader. "I haven't decided yet," she answered, eating another potato chip.

"I'll take that as a 'yes'," Myrtle said with a smile. She finished the rest of her lunch just as Chandler was finishing hers. "Okay, my dear Chandler, I have things to do and you have to get back to work." She looked up at the younger woman, smiling and saying, "But for what it's worth, your parents and grandma would approve."

Chandler just looked at her and tried not to tear up. "Thank you," was all she could say.

They packed up their trash and threw it away. Myrtle put her arm around Chandler as they walked out of the park. "You are very special, and I love seeing you happy," she said.

"I know that, Myrtle. I'm grateful every day to have you, Rosie, and all the other ladies in my life." They were the closest thing to a family she had.

"Oh, speaking of Rosie," Myrtle said as they were entering the bakery, "she'll be eighty-four next week and we were thinking it would be nice to have a birthday dinner for her at the Hilltop. If we have it there, Andrea won't feel compelled to work, giving her a nice break."

"When were you thinking?" asked Chandler. She hoped she wasn't going to say Wednesday.

"Saturday evening. All the graduation stuff is over now, so we should be able to get the small side room that will seat around twenty. I was going to invite all the ladies of the group, and they could all bring a guest." Myrtle stopped and looked directly at Chandler and said, "Of course, please ask Peter, since it is his grandmother."

"Okay, I'll say something to him. He's going to be calling later today. Do you want me to make a cake for Rosie?" Chandler brought out the cake she had been working on earlier, from the cooler and set it on the decorating counter.

Myrtle smiled. "Of course dear. That is a beautiful cake. Is it for Vivian Granderson?"

Chandler had to smile because Myrtle really did know everything about everyone in Hope Springs. "Yes, do you think she'll like it?"

"Oh, she'll love it! It looks just like a basket of flowers," Myrtle said, excitedly. "Hey, do you think you could make one for Rosie that looks like a quilt?"

"Sure I can. I'll ask MaryAnn to get me a picture of the quilt we just finished and go from there," Chandler answered.

"Okay, I'll get the room set up and the girls will help with the rest," Myrtle said, excitedly. "This is going to be one fantastic party!"

Chapter 28

Chandler stood looking at the dresses in her closet. "Everything is either too dressy, meant for church, or winter," she said out loud, moving the hangers from side to side. She needed something soft and casual, yet cool for summer, for her dinner with Peter the following night. Chandler looked over at the bedside clock. "I better get moving, or I'm going to be late." She laughed at the fact that she was talking to herself.

Chandler grabbed her purse, and headed out the front door, locking it behind her. As she walked out into the warm Virginia morning, she breathed in deeply. She could smell the freshly mown grass from her neighbor across the street. As she walked, she could smell the heavenly scent of the rose hedge another neighbor painstakingly kept perfectly straight up and down and across the top. "Hmmm," she sighed as she passed.

As Chandler came up to Main Street and waited to cross over to the bakery, she saw Hillary walking with her little ones. "Good morning, Hillary," Chandler greeted her friend. "And how are you all this morning?" Chandler longed for the day she had a family of her own.

"Oh, you know," Hillary began, "the natives are a little restless this morning." She smiled and continued, "They need to burn off a little energy before I take them to Jack's mom for the day. We were just headed to the park for a bit. At least it's big enough for them to run around."

"I hadn't thought about the fact that we don't have a playground close to downtown," Chandler said, looking at Hillary's sweet children.

Hillary shrugged her shoulders. "It would be helpful not to have to walk all the way to the elementary school, that's for sure. I wonder who we need to talk to about possibly getting something on this side of town?"

"I would suspect the town council would be the place to start," Chandler proposed.

"Maybe this revitalization plan everyone is talking about also includes a playground," Hillary suggested, as her children grew more restless standing around waiting for their mother to finish her conversation. "I'd better get moving or they'll mutiny."

Before Hillary walked away, Chandler said, "I was going to stop by your shop later today. I'm looking for a couple of cute sundresses for summer."

"Any particular reason?" Hillary asked, smiling.

"Maybe," Chandler hedged.

"I'll have Missy pull some stuff and have it ready when you come by," Hillary told her. "How about after the morning rush?"

"I'll be over around 10:30. Now get those kids to the park quickly," Chandler said, laughing at the kids getting louder in their pleas for their mom to hurry up.

"See you then," Hillary yelled back as she was being dragged away by her three little ones.

Once again, the thought cross her mind of what it would be like to have children of her own. *Let's not go down that road, Chandler,* she admonished herself. *How about a second date, first.*

"Good morning, Chandler," Gretchen greeted her boss a short time later. "Luann is running a little late this morning. She said something about needing to make sure her classes are all lined up for the fall."

"Oh, I forgot she mentioned that to me yesterday," Chandler remembered, hurrying to get the coffee started. "I'm sorry, I'm late. I was going through my wardrobe and lost track of time. Then I ran into Hillary and her kids. They are the sweetest little ones." Chandler didn't realize she was rambling on until she saw Gretchen stop what she was doing and look at her.

"A little busy already this morning, are we?" Gretchen asked with a grin. "Why the sudden need to go through your wardrobe?"

Chandler grinned and said, "just trying to see if I have anything between dresses that I used to wear for the gallery openings and dresses for church."

"And is there a *reason* you need to have that particular type of dress?" Gretchen asked, knowing full well the answer to her question.

Chandler pretended to fix the tie on the back of her apron. "Sometimes a girl just wants to wear a casual sundress in the summer, that's all."

"Oh, so you'll be wearing this sundress to work?" Gretchen teased.

"Maybe," Chandler answered, as the phone rang, saving her from the rest of this line of questioning. "Sweet Stuff Bakery, Chandler speaking," Chandler answered. She went on to take a birthday cake order as Gretchen got back to work stocking the cases.

Later, after the morning rush, Chandler headed over to Hillary's shop, amid the teasing from both Gretchen and Luann.

"Oh good, you're here," Missy said as Chandler walked in the front door. "I hope you like what I've picked out for you. Come on back to the dressing room and see what you think."

Chandler followed Missy to the back of the shop as Hillary was coming out of the back room. "Hi Chandler," Hillary greeted her friend. "I've seen what Missy has picked out for you, and I think she missed her calling. She should be a personal stylist."

"I hope you like these," Missy told Chandler, pointing to the three dresses hanging on the hooks inside the small dressing room. "I'll leave you to try them on," she said as she pulled the door closed.

Chandler looked at each of the dresses Missy had picked out. She honestly loved all three of them. Starting with the first dress, she put it on and came out to look in the three-way mirror. This one was a mint green tea-length dress with spaghetti straps and a sweetheart neckline. The dress flared out at the waist, and swirled at her calf. "I love this," Chandler gushed as she looked at herself in the mirror.

"That one looks terrific on you," Hillary agreed. "I think someone would like it very much," she added, smiling.

"Very funny," Chandler remarked. "Okay, this is fun. Let's try another one." It had been such a long time since Chandler had bought anything other than jeans and t-shirts.

Next, she tried on a navy sleeveless shirt dress that was fitted at the waist and flared at the hips. "You know, I wasn't sure if I was going to like this one," she remarked, coming out of the dressing room, "but it's kind of growing on me."

Missy looked at the dress. "It needs a little something," she said, tapping her finger to her lips. "I know! I'll be right back." Chandler watched as Missy rushed to the front window and took a silver metallic belt of one of the mannequins. "Here, let's try this," she said as she wrapped the belt around Chandler's slender waist. "Perfect," Missy declared.

"Missy, I think Hillary is right," Chandler said as she stared at herself in the mirror. "You really should be a personal stylist."

"I enjoy helping women feel good about themselves," Missy replied. "Now let's see if we're three for three."

Chandler tried on the third dress, which was a pale pink sheath dress. "It's not as casual as the other two," she said, "but it would be great for an evening out. Missy, I'd say you could be my personal stylist any day."

"Should we wrap these up for you?" Hillary asked as before Chandler headed back into the dressing room to change from the last dress.

"Yep," Chandler told her. "I'll pay for them now, and pick them up on my way home from the bakery, if that's okay with you." She didn't want any more teasing from Gretchen and Luann.

"Sure," Hillary agreed, "we're open late tonight until 8:00."

Chandler left Hillary's shop feeling like a new person. Sometimes all a woman needed was a few new dresses to make herself feel beautiful.

Chapter 29

Wednesday morning Chandler woke up excited for the day. The workload at the bakery was light since it was mid-week, so she had told Gretchen and Luann she would only be in for a short time, but they could call if they needed her.

Chandler decided to go to the grocery store out by the highway, because she needed the pork roast and trimmings that she knew she couldn't get at Fran's mercantile. She was looking over the produce to pick just the right vegetables when she overheard two women she recognized as wives of town council members. They were discussing the revitalization project, so Chandler stopped to listen in.

"Larry said he couldn't believe the mayor was going to just let that developer demolish several blocks in the historic district," Freda said.

"I know," agreed Sylvia. "My George said he figured that young blonde must be doing something with the mayor, if you know what I mean, to get him to agree to this."

Freda replied, "That's what Larry said last night. Luckily, they all have to vote on it before it goes through. I think if it were up to the mayor it would have already been done. Larry is hoping they can vote against it and stop this madness."

Sylvia agreed. "I don't know why we have to revitalize anyway. The town is fine just the way it is."

As their conversation turned to other topics, Chandler made a mental note to check with Myrtle about just who this blonde woman was before it hit her like a ton of bricks. *Was this the same blonde woman I practically ran into at Peter's?* she thought, feeling a little sick to her stomach. She hoped her first intuition was wrong and he wasn't involved with all this. Besides, there were thousands of blonde women in the world. Chandler decided to put that on the back burner for now. She was so looking forward to their evening, and didn't want anything to ruin it.

Chandler finished her shopping and headed back to her place. She put her groceries away and put the pork roast in the oven. It would take about six hours to cook it low and slow. She looked up at the clock and saw that it was lunchtime. She decided to go up to Andrea's for a bite to eat and pick up the apple pie she had ordered.

She walked into the diner and saw the mayor having lunch, so she decided to do a little sleuthing herself. "Hello, Mayor Thompson. How are you today?" she asked with a forced smile.

The mayor put his fork down long enough to say, "Just fine, Chandler. How is the bakery doing? Seemed a little slow this morning."

Chandler didn't realize the mayor cared so much about her business. "Oh, Wednesdays are usually a little slower than the rest of the week. Any other day it's all we can do to keep up."

"Oh, I was under the impression things weren't going well," he said, snidely.

"Now, sir, what would give you that impression?" Chandler said, somewhat defensively. "Nothing could be further from the truth."

Now it was his turn to get defensive. "Oh, I don't remember exactly where I heard it. I'm glad it's not true." Was it her imagination or was he getting just a bit uncomfortable with this conversation? Chandler decided to fish some more.

"How is the bidding for the revitalization project going? How many firms have submitted bids so far?" Chandler asked.

Now he really was squirming. "Oh, well, I'm not allowed to discuss official business with the residents. That is private government business."

"Really?" asked Chandler, smiling. "Because people are talking about your 'official business' all over town. From what I've heard, you've already decided on a firm." She leaned down to make sure he heard the next part. "Just remember, you need approval from the town council, after a public hearing, before anything can be decided."

The fact that Chandler knew so much about the workings of town government took the mayor totally by surprise. "Just what makes you an expert in town government?" he asked, all high and mighty.

"High school government class," was her answer. "Have a good lunch." And with that she walked away, leaving him and his tablemates staring in disbelief.

Chandler saw that Macy and MaryAnn were seated in a booth along the wall motioning for her to join them.

"What was *that* all about?" asked MaryAnn, as Chandler sat down.

"Oh, I heard a rumor that the mayor had already decided on a developer without approval from the town council or a public hearing. I just wanted to make sure he knew that someone was watching him," Chandler explained as she looked over the menu.

The waitress came to take their orders. "Man, Chandler, I don't know what you said to the mayor, but he is hot under the collar over it. I've never seen him this red before, except when Andrea made three-alarm chili and forgot to warn him about how hot it was."

"Good. It's about time someone held him accountable," MaryAnn said. "Sometimes I think he has forgotten he's an elected official and he works for us."

"Well, now he knows he's being watched," Chandler told her. "Maybe he won't try and pull a fast one on the town. We do have rights, and I intend to make sure we exercise said rights."

After they had all ordered lunch, they talked about how exciting it was going to be having Rosie's eighty-fourth birthday party on Saturday night.

"Are you going to ask Peter to come?" asked Macy, as the waitress delivered their beverages.

"Yes, Myrtle made sure I would," replied Chandler, peeling the paper from her straw and placing the straw in her glass.

"Any details yet on Dr. Howard's replacement, Macy?" asked MaryAnn, pouring two packets of sweetener into her tea.

"His name is Dr. Grainger. He's from the city and is finishing up his residency, but that's all I've heard. He's coming to meet all of us on Friday," Macy told them. Chandler noticed Macy was nervously playing with her hair and wondered if it had anything to do with the new doctor. She chose not to ask with MaryAnn present.

The waitress brought out their lunches and Chandler answered their questions about her Saturday night with Peter. She stopped short of telling them Peter was coming for dinner. Once their bills had been paid and Chandler had her pre-ordered apple pie, they said their goodbyes.

Chapter 30

Chandler walked the rest of the way home feeling quite proud of the way she acted with the mayor. *What a jerk!* she thought. *How dare he think my business is not doing well based solely on one Wednesday morning? I wonder what he'd have done if I'd mentioned the blonde woman? That could have gotten really interesting.*

She spent the afternoon sprucing up the house and getting her dinner pulled together. At about 5:00 p.m., she showered and changed into the mint green sundress she had purchased at Hillary's. She left her hair long, because Peter had said he liked it that way, and put on a little make-up. At about 6:20 p.m., she heard a knock at the door announcing his arrival. She loved a man who was prompt or even a little early.

As she opened the front door, it struck her just how handsome Peter Frederick really was. "Hello, and welcome to my home," she greeted him with a smile.

Peter entered and looked around. "This is fabulous," he gushed, really meaning it.

"Thanks," she said, smiling. "I love it."
"Maybe I should have paid you to decorate my condo," he said, looking around her living room, which was small, but not cramped. "Your place actually looks like a home, not a mausoleum." He saw

that she had little mementos from her childhood scattered around the room.

"Oh, stop," she said, laughing. "Your place has a great view, even if it is a little gray," she teased, as she watched him walk over to the shelf holding photos of her and her family.

"I'd much rather live in a place like this. Who cares about the view if the rest of the place isn't a home," he remarked, looking at the photos of a younger Chandler. He realized at that moment that he didn't have any of these things. He was sure there were photos and mementos of his somewhere. But in order to see where, Peter knew he'd have to speak to the man he hadn't spoken to since his mother's funeral.

He put that thought on the back burner and turned to Chandler. "You look beautiful," he commented, looking at her sundress. "And whatever you're cooking smells fantastic." Chandler took his hand and led him back to the kitchen. "Even the kitchen is homey," he remarked. Peter had grown up with a housekeeper who was more like a surrogate parent. His parents were more concerned about their business and life at the country club than in what he was doing.

"Surely your kitchen was like this growing up?" Chandler asked, somewhat surprised by his reaction.

"Well, you know the saying about the kitchen being the heart of the home?" he asked. When she nodded, he answered, "not for everyone."

Chandler felt sorry for the boy who didn't grow up in a loving environment. "Surely your parents loved you," she said, not knowing quite what to say to that.

Peter smiled. "Don't get me wrong, I did all the things kids I grew up with did. I played sports in school, went to dances, all that stuff. But my parents were too busy working and going to the country club with friends to attend any of my events." He stopped and shrugged. "My way wasn't bad, just different." He wanted to make sure Chandler knew his upbringing wasn't terrible by any stretch of the imagination.

"I agree, just different," Chandler said to him. "It was what you knew, like living here in Hope Springs was what I knew." Her parents and grandparents had attended every one of her events growing up. She couldn't imagine looking out into the audience of one of her plays, or out into the stands at one of her games and not seeing them.

Peter thought about that statement. "I'm beginning to think I would have liked growing up in Hope Springs better than growing up in the city."

"I think both have their good and bad," Chandler surmised. "For instance, I would have set the table outside on the deck, but then we would be on full display."

"And?" Peter asked, not following her.

"And Mabel lives behind me, and you know what would happen then," Chandler explained, both of them knowing full well Mabel would be calling Myrtle as soon as they were spotted. "So, for now, we'll eat inside. Maybe, if we feel brave after dinner, we can have dessert on the front porch and I can show you off to the neighbors."

"Show me off?" he questioned, hands on his hips. "What am I, your prized bull?" he teased.

Chandler chuckled and handed him the bottle of wine she had picked up to go with dinner. "Would you mind pouring us each a glass while I get dinner on the table? I hope you like pork roast, mashed potatoes, and green beans," she said as she opened the oven door to retrieve the roast and mashed potatoes she'd already prepared ahead of time.

"Oh, my," Peter sighed. "I'll have to work extra hard at the gym tomorrow," he declared, patting his stomach.

"Make that extra, extra hard. We have apple pie for dessert," she informed him. "Though I can't take credit for the pie; it came from Andrea's."

They sat down to eat and Peter lavished her with praise for the best meal he had eaten in a very long time. "No, really, probably the last time I had a dinner like this was at my Grandmother Rosie's when I was a little boy."

Chandler thought that was more than a little sad. "Speaking of Rosie, we're celebrating her eighty-fourth birthday on Saturday night at the Hilltop. I kid you not, I was literally ordered to invite you. If you don't come, I fear the Little Old Lady Network will probably attack me," she teased with a grin.

"Well, far be it from me to make them mad at you," Peter replied with a wink. "Count me in."

Chandler noticed how easy it was to carry on a conversation with Peter. Nothing seemed forced or rehearsed. It was nice to be able to talk about her day without being made to feel that her day wasn't important. Peter seemed genuinely interested in everything she had to say.

"Macy mentioned today that someone named Dr. Grainger is taking over for Dr. Howard. She said he's coming Friday to meet everyone."

Peter looked at her, an unreadable expression on his handsome face. "Really? I know a Dr. Jake Grainger. I wonder if it's any relation."

"Apparently he is going to take over for Dr. Howard when he retires from the medical center, and he will be the new town doc. How do you know your Dr. Grainger?" she asked.

He smiled a big smile. "He's my best friend," he answered proudly.

Now it was Chandler's turn to stare at him in surprise. "You don't think it's the same person, do you? Wouldn't your best friend have mentioned if he were moving to Hope Springs?" Chandler knew that men didn't talk about personal things to each other nearly as much as women, but this was a life-changing career move.

Peter shook his head. "You'd think so, but you can bet I'll be asking him about it when I see him at the gym tomorrow morning."

Once they were finished with what Peter kept referring to as "the best meal he'd ever eaten," they decided it was probably safe to have their dessert on the front porch. They worked together to clean up the kitchen, complete with loading the dishwasher and handwashing whatever didn't fit. Again, something none of Chandler's previous boyfriends ever even volunteered to help with. By then it was about 8:15 or so, and darkness was descending on Hope Springs.

"We can sit on the porch in the dark and no one will know we're there," Chandler said as they were getting their dessert and after-dinner coffee.

Peter picked up the tray containing their dessert and coffee and asked her to lead the way. They made their way out onto the front porch and took a seat on the small outdoor glider. "This is so nice," he stated, after he had put the tray on the small table in front of the glider, "so quiet and peaceful."

"A little more quiet than where you live, huh." Chandler nudged him with her elbow, as she handed him his coffee and pie.

"Just a bit," he answered, smelling the flowers in the soft summer breeze. He could imagine this was what it was like when people referred to the 'sleepy little town where the sidewalks were rolled up at night'. He was pleasantly surprised how easy it was to just sit here with Chandler. She was the only woman he'd ever known who didn't constantly want to be doing something, usually when his money was involved. His own mother hadn't been like this; he didn't even know this type of woman existed. And he was pleasantly surprised he was okay with just sitting.

They ate their pie in comfortable silence, listening to the quiet sounds of a summer night. They could see in the distance that a group of kids were playing flashlight tag, while a dog was barking down the street. They could hear the frogs croaking from near the lake, and a slight rustling of the wind in the leaves. To Chandler this was heaven on earth. She hoped it was the same for Peter.

As if reading her mind, he took their plates and placed them on the tray, then he put his arm around her and whispered, "This is so relaxing. A guy could get used to this."

Chandler put her head on his shoulder and they sat swaying on the glider. All was right with her world, and Chandler hoped this feeling would never end.

Chapter 31

"So how did you end up getting the job to replace Dr. Howard in Hope Springs?" Peter asked Jake between breaths as they were running on the treadmills the next morning. He had really enjoyed his time with Chandler, and they had stayed on the porch until almost 11:00 p.m. talking and laughing. He had left her and made the drive home, finally crawling into bed sometime after midnight. Even though he didn't want to meet Jake at the gym that morning, he'd forced himself to get up and go.

"Oh, that's right, your grandmother lives in Hope Springs," Jake replied. "It all happened pretty quickly. Someone at the hospital mentioned Dr. Howard was retiring, and frankly I'm ready for a change of pace. I went down to interview with him and he hired me on the spot." Jake told Peter he loved the small town, and the change in atmosphere from the city. It wasn't a hard decision to make.

Peter knew what Jake meant; Hope Springs was quickly becoming his favorite place. "So when do you start?"

"I'm going down tomorrow to meet the staff. I need to find a place to live as well," Jake explained. "The plan is to start in about a month. I'll be shadowing Dr. Howard for a couple of weeks to meet his patients. He's planning to be fully retired by the end of the summer."

"So that means you'll be an official small town doctor," said Peter. "Will you also be making house calls?" He didn't even know if that was a thing anymore.

"Not sure," answered Jake, shrugging his shoulders, not sure if Peter was joking. "So how are things going with Chandler?" he asked, changing the subject.

Peter smiled, "Great, I think. We had dinner at her place last night. Her house is so much more of a home than mine. I never thought of myself as the type who could sit on a porch glider for three hours and not move, but that's what we did. I think I could get used to that."

"Does she know what you do for a living?" asked Jake.

"She knows I'm a developer," Peter answered, "but not that I'm the developer in charge of the Hope Springs revitalization project."

Jake shook his head. "That's a slippery slope, my friend. What are you going to do if she finds out?"

"I have an alternative plan beginning to form," Peter explained. "As long as I can keep Cassia from finding out *that* plan and spilling the beans before I'm ready, everything should work out fine." He knew however, it was a big risk to try and keep secrets. But the reward may be far greater than the risk, if it meant having Chandler in his life.

"Oh, yes, and how is your assistant?" Jake inquired, referring to Cassia.

"Still trying to make the relationship more than business," Peter told him. Peter knew he was really running out of time to get his plan for Hope Springs lined up. If Cassia decided to make a move with the mayor before Peter was ready, then his relationship with Chandler very well might be over. And Chandler had made it clear she didn't like people who lied to her. He certainly didn't blame her for that.

"Well, for your sake let's hope that doesn't happen," Jake cautioned as they headed toward the showers.

Peter walked into his office a little while later and found Cassia sitting in his chair. "Good morning. May I help you with something, Cassia?" he asked, annoyed to find her in his office.

"Hello, I was just waiting for you so could I let you know the time for the meeting with the mayor," she said, standing up and smoothing her dress over her hips.

Peter noticed that once again she was wearing a tight dress, a little too high above the knee, and four inch heels. *She must not have anything else in her closet,* he thought as he fought the urge to roll his eyes. He walked around her and sat in his chair. "Okay, when is it?"

"I have scheduled our meeting with Mayor Thompson for noon, next Friday," she answered, leaning against his desk. "He wants to have a lunch meeting at the Hilltop Restaurant. I figured you and I could ride together," she said, brightly.

Peter was glad to have an entire week to get his new proposal ready to present, because there was no way he was presenting the current one. There were too many people he cared about who would be affected. "I'll have Pat put it on my calendar, but we'll take two cars," he said, opening the top file on the stack on his desk. He figured that as soon as she heard his proposal, she'd hit the roof, and he didn't want to be in the same car with her after she did.

Cassia put on her best pouty face. "But that would be such a waste of gas. I think we should ride together."

"Expense your gas," he answered, not bothering to look up from the file, hopefully giving her the impression that their conversation was over.

"Oh, alright," she pouted, as she sauntered out of his office.

Cassia walked back to her office thinking that something just didn't add up on the Hope Springs Project. She didn't understand why Peter was suddenly interested in every aspect.

She sat down at her desk and pulled out the file of additional photos she'd had taken of the area, but hadn't shown to Peter. She leaned back in her chair and carefully looked over each one. When she came to the photo taken of the bakery, her red nail tapped on the photo of the woman behind the counter. She sat straight up and realized the woman in the photo was the same woman she had run into at Peter's condo! *Old friends, my eye!* She thought. *No wonder Peter had such a sudden interest. One of the businesses belongs to his new girlfriend!*

Cassia leaned back in her chair and tapped her nail to her lips. There was no way she was going to let the baker be the reason this multi-million-dollar deal was destroyed, and she certainly wasn't going to stand by and let that woman take Peter away from her. Somehow she had to take care of this.

Just then her phone rang, nearly making her jump out of her seat. As she answered it, the answer to her problem spoke across the other end of the line. She finished her conversation and hung up, leaning back to tap her nails on the desk. A big smile spread across her impeccably glossed lips. *Perfect,* she thought.

Chapter 32

Thursday evening Rosie and MaryAnn were admiring the red, white, and blue star, full-size quilt they had loaded on the frame earlier in the day. As always, MaryAnn had marked the lines for everyone to follow. Since Katrina Smith would not be coming home until August, they had approximately six weeks to complete the quilt.

"MaryAnn, I love the way you made the quilt design swirl and feather around the stars," Rosie said. "It will really make them pop."

"I was looking for something that would make it a little more feminine, since our service member is a woman. When you make a red, white, and blue quilt with stars, it can tend to go toward the manlier side," MaryAnn explained.

Rosie lightly brushed her hand over the quilt. "I think Katrina is going to love it. I was so happy to hear her wounds were not too severe, so she won't have to spend too much time in the hospital. I know her family is going to be happy when she's home." Rosie had spoken to Katrina's parents at church on several occasions, and knew what an ordeal it had been for the entire family.

Everyone started arriving and soon all were sitting around with big plates of salad and bread. Since it was late June, a cold salad was a good choice on a hot summer evening. Admiration for the newest project was evident.

"God bless Katrina for all she has gone through," Andrea said quietly. "I'm not sure I'd have been that strong."

Rosie patted her hand. "You've been through your own brand of hell and you came out just fine," she said, knowing all Andrea had endured watching her husband succumb to cancer. "I don't think you give yourself enough credit." Andrea just smiled.

"So, Macy," Myrtle said, turning to the young woman, "What's our new town doc like?"

Macy smiled, "I don't know. I get to meet him tomorrow when he comes to meet the staff. My guess is he's probably some doctor in his fifties."

"I don't think so," said Chandler, taking a bite of her bread.

Myrtle turned to her. "Oh, have you met him?"

"No," Chandler replied, "but if it's the same Dr. Grainger I'm thinking of, he's Peter's best friend, so I don't think he's in his fifties."
"Speaking of Peter," Myrtle said slyly, "I hear you had him over to your house for dinner last night. Apparently, he didn't leave until after 11:00."

Chandler just rolled her eyes. She knew she couldn't keep that a secret, but as Myrtle didn't actually ask a direct question, Chandler chose not to respond. She looked over at Rosie who was giving her a look as if to say she was pleased with where the relationship with Peter was going, and if Chandler didn't want to divulge details, she didn't have to. Chandler knew Rosie was one who didn't pry, and got frustrated with Myrtle when she did.

Fran was the one to break the silence. "How was your evening, Chandler?"

197

Chandler got up to throw her empty dinner dishes away and get a cookie from the platter she had brought. "It was lovely," was all she would say. She sat back down and waited for the onslaught from Myrtle. To her immense surprise, it never came.

"I'm so happy for you, Chandler," said Fran, smiling. "You've really had some losers in the past, and it sounds like you've finally found a winner."

"Definitely," MaryAnn agreed. "Sometimes you need to weed out the wrong men until you find the right one."

Chandler thought about what MaryAnn had said. Had she really found the right one? How could one possibly know that? There was no manual on the characteristics of what the 'right one' was. "MaryAnn, how do you know if he's the right one?" she asked.

"Well, for me, it was when Robert went off to college. I couldn't wait for him to come home on break. Back then, there weren't cell phones and email, so our communication was limited to long distance calls and letters," explained MaryAnn.

"Wow," whispered Macy, "no emails or anything?"

"No," replied MaryAnn with a wink, "not back in the olden days."

"I know you younger ladies rely heavily on your cell phones for texting and email for communication," said Rosie, "but writing letters and talking on the phone was so much more personal. A lot can be misunderstood in a text message."

"Definitely," agreed Fran, smoothing her peasant blouse over her skirt. "Can you imagine the text message I would have received if my ex had decided to inform me of our breakup via text instead of calling from his girlfriend's house? I don't think my fingers would have been able to keep up with all the names I was calling him over the phone. I may have caught it on fire!" she said, laughing.

"So, to answer your question," MaryAnn said to Chandler, "you'll just know. When you're thinking about him all the time or when you wake up in the morning and your first thought is about him, you'll know, and you'll feel wonderful and excited and scared all at the same time."

"Wow, this was productive dinner conversation," concluded Rosie. "Let's start working on this quilt." Everyone started cleaning up the dinner dishes and took their places around the quilt frame.

As they sat and began stitching the beautiful feathered design, Chandler looked around at the ladies in the group. Each and every one of them meant so much to her, and she knew they all cared as much for her. It was so nice to have such a support group. She knew that if she ever needed help, they'd all come running.

Chapter 33

Saturday morning the bakery was so busy, Chandler, Gretchen, and Luann never even had time to take a break. Chandler hoped the mayor was doing his usual walk around town to see that her place was swamped with customers from open to close. She hated for him to think her business was in trouble, when nothing could be further from the truth.

By 3:00 p.m., they had sold almost everything in the cases. Gretchen was finishing up the last cake order just as the customer came in to pick it up. Chandler then boxed up the cake she had made for Rosie's birthday party. She was quite proud of the rectangular cake with a quilt design on it. It was done in a pale pink, yellow, and lavender patchwork design. The center was reserved for "Happy 84th Rosie" written in dark pink to stand out against the pale colors in the quilt blocks.

They all worked together to close the shop so they could go home and get ready for the party. Chandler swung by the Hilltop Restaurant to deliver Rosie's cake on her way home.

She made it home in plenty of time to take a shower and put on her new light green sundress before Peter came to meet her for the party. As the time was getting near for him to arrive, she grew more and more excited at the thought of seeing him again. Maybe this was what MaryAnn was talking about – she just couldn't wait to see him again.

The doorbell rang, and when she opened it and took in his smile, she knew. "Hello," she answered with a smile.

"Hi, yourself," Peter said, stepping in the door and closing it. She stepped into his warm embrace and welcomed his kiss.

He reluctantly released her and moved back a step. "I've missed you," he murmured huskily, running a hand down the side of her cheek.

"I've missed you, too," she whispered with a shy smile, realizing that she truly meant it.

"I'm not sure where this is going," he said, as he tenderly brushed the hair back from her face, "but I like the direction."

"Me too," she whispered against his lips before he kissed her again. As her head started to spin, she pulled away once more with a rueful smile. "I guess we better get going."

"I guess so," he said. "Don't want to be late for my own grandmother's party."

He opened the door and they both stepped out into the evening sunshine. He held her hand as they walked up to the Hilltop. Chandler figured that since everyone in town knew he had been at her house on Wednesday, they really had nothing to hide anymore.

When they got to the Hilltop, they realized that they were the last ones to arrive. Much to Chandler's blushing dismay, upon seeing them arrive together, the ladies of the group serenaded them with a chorus of whistles and catcalls.

Peter walked over to Rosie and gathered her in for a big hug. "Happy birthday, Grandmother," he greeted her.

"Oh, Peter, I'm so glad you could make it," Rosie said. "And Chandler, the cake is perfect! Thank you so much for making it."

"Only the best for you, Rosie," Chandler said, hugging her. "Happy birthday."

They took their seats next to Rosie while Myrtle informed the group that the buffet would be ready in a couple of minutes. "Chat amongst yourselves and work up an appetite in the meantime," she said.

They had just placed their drink orders with the waiter when Chandler looked up and saw a familiar face marching toward them from across the restaurant.

"Peter, there is that woman we ran into at your condo," she whispered, shocked to see her in Hope Springs.

Peter looked up and saw Cassia coming toward them, with perhaps the snidest expression he'd ever seen crossing her face. What in the world was she doing in Hope Springs?!

"Hello, Peter," Cassia called out loudly. "What a surprise to see you here."

The rest of the group turned to see the owner of the shrill voice invading their party. "Oh, no," Myrtle nudged Fran, "this can't be good." This was the same woman everyone had seen with the mayor recently.

Peter stood up. "Hi, Cassia. Yes, this is quite the surprise. I'm here for my grandmother's eighty-fourth birthday," he said, sternly. "What brings you to Hope Springs?"

"Oh, the mayor and his wife invited me for dinner. He wanted me to fill her in on the details of the revitalization project," she answered loud enough for the whole table to hear. "If I'd known you were going to be here, I'd have invited you as well since it is *your* company that will be doing the project." She wanted to make it very clear to the baker just who Peter was.

"What?" asked Myrtle in disbelief. "Peter, your company is in charge? You lied to all of us?"

"Cassia," Peter began, holding up a finger to the group as if to say, *wait a minute*, "nothing has been finalized. I haven't even met the mayor yet. I thought we weren't meeting with him until next week."

"Oh, that's just a formality, Peter. He loved the entire concept." She waved him off, sidestepping his statement about meeting the following week. "Demolishing two blocks on each side of Main Street and building two, four-story office buildings in their place."

"Two blocks!" Myrtle shouted. "Which two blocks?"

Cassia tapped her finger against her cheek. "The two blocks where the boutique, post office, and visitor's center are. As well as the bakery and library across the street, of course," she finished, as if that were a very silly question to ask. "Those buildings are all but falling down already. So, it's no big deal."

"It may not be a big deal to you," Hillary argued, "but one of those buildings is my business, my husband's business, and our home." Cassia had the nerve to just look at her with a smug look on her face. Hillary wanted to shake that look off Cassia's face! *How dare she demean all that Jack and I have worked so hard for,* Hillary thought.

"But I thought the town council would have to vote on any proposed plan," Macy stated, confused by what was going on. "Isn't that right, Chandler?"

Chandler didn't answer, but sat there in a state of utter shock. *This can't be happening,* she thought. *It has to be a dream; no, a nightmare. I'm going to wake up any minute now.* But that wasn't the case.

"That's right," agreed Hillary. "There has to be a public hearing, as well."

Cassia continued, "Well ladies, your mayor said he makes all the decisions and the council will do whatever he wishes."

"Not if we impeach him!" Myrtle all but shouted. All of a sudden there was a cacophony of noise as all the women started commenting at once.

"Peter," Rosie interrupted, aghast. "Please tell me that's not the plan. Please tell me you aren't going to destroy half this town."

"Grandmother, I can explain," he started, before Cassia interrupted.

"Hi, there. Rosie, is it?" She asked with a sickly, sweet smile as she held out her hand, "Happy birthday."

Rosie, who was usually the queen of manners and decorum, chose not to shake her hand or acknowledge her presence, sniffing and turning her head. "Peter, please explain."

"When the idea for this project came across my desk, I had no idea how much history was in this town," Peter tried to explain, "I haven't even met the mayor yet, and it seems that Cassia has been going behind my back to make this deal. I'm still in a bit of a shock myself." Peter now knew what it felt to be blindsided and seeing red. He had never been madder at anyone in his life than he was at Cassia at this very moment.

"Oh, dear, well I can see I've caused quite the interruption to your party," Cassia said with false sincerity. "I'll let you get back to your celebration." Cassia turned on her heel, shooting Chandler a narrowed glare before she sauntered back across the room to her table with a satisfied smile on her face.

In the deafening silence that followed, everyone turned and looked at Chandler, who had yet to say a word. *The bakery,* she thought, *I'm going to lose my bakery.* She was stunned, heartbroken, and speechless all in one. All she could do was look up at Peter with a glazed expression. As if struck by lightning, her feet were suddenly in motion, and before she knew it she was up and out the door, having paused to drop a kiss on Rosie's cheek.

Peter got up to go after her before Rosie stopped him with a hand on his arm. "Leave her for now, Peter. I think I'd like for you to take me home now. I'm suddenly not in the mood for a party."

Myrtle spoke up, "Mr. Frederick, I'm not sure what just happened here, but I do know that you have probably just lost the best woman you will ever meet." She turned to Rosie and gave her a hug. "Don't worry about all this birthday stuff, I'll take care of it. You see if you can talk some sense into your grandson." She turned back to Peter, shaking her arthritic finger at him. "The way to a good woman's heart is definitely not by tearing down her business, young man."

Peter turned toward the group with a pleading expression, "That was never my intention. I will fix this and I will get Chandler to believe in me again." He held out his hand for Rosie. "Come on Grandmother, I'll take you home."

After they had left, Myrtle said to the remaining party guests, "I'm not giving up on that boy just yet. Maybe he can fix this." She walked across the dining room to address the blonde who'd crashed the party. "I don't know who you are, but I do know you've managed to hurt a lot of people I care about. If I were you, I'd stay out of Hope Springs from now on."

Cassia put her hand to her chest, feigning shock. "Old woman, is that a threat?"

Myrtle just smiled. "Nope, it's a promise." She turned her back on the too done-up blonde and walked back across the room with a plan of her own. "Fran, come with me. We have work to do."

"Uh oh," Fran said, getting up from her chair. "I know that look."

Chapter 34

Peter and Rosie walked out of the restaurant, but instead of heading toward her home, Rosie turned and walked toward the War Memorial. As Peter followed, Rosie walked past the buildings set to be demolished. She took a long moment to stop in front of each one, studying its features carefully, soaking in the cooling night air and listening to the sounds of Hope Springs at night. They crossed to the middle of the circle where the War Memorial stood.

"You know, Peter, your ancestors' names are on this Memorial," she stated, looking at the bronze statue of a soldier from long ago. The names of their ancestors and many others who lost their lives fighting in wars were inscribed on the marble base.

The sound of the American flag flapping in the breeze, lit up twenty-four hours a day as a reminder of the sacrifice of those same men, caused Peter to look up toward the sky. "Yes, I know," he replied, turning his gaze down to look at the names. Peter wasn't sure where she was going with this, but he was sure there was some kind of lesson he needed to hear.

Rosie turned around and faced the town. "They were fighting for this," she said, as she raised her hands toward the town, "and so will I."

Peter knew exactly what she was saying. She, *no*, he thought, *they* were a part of the history of this town. Heritage meant everything to Rosie and the other women of this town, and they would use whatever means necessary to preserve it. He really had to admire their determination and the profound love they all shared for each other and their community. Those were qualities he was lacking in his own life. He wondered, not for the first time, what it would be like to live in Hope Springs.

With that, Rosie started walking back toward her home. Instead of going down Main Street, she turned and walked up the next block over, behind the library and bakery. He followed. They walked past the church where she worshiped every Sunday, and where generations of their family had before her. "You should come to a service someday, Peter. It might do you good to spend some time with God," she said.

She didn't wait for him to answer; she just kept on walking. They walked past the back of the hardware store and by the back of the Hilltop Restaurant. As they turned left to go to Rosie's house, Peter noticed Myrtle and Fran around a familiar little red sports car in the parking lot behind the Hilltop. He only needed one guess to figure out what they might be up to. A hint of a smile came across his face. Myrtle was one ornery lady.

Once they got to Rosie's, she ordered him to have a seat on the porch and said she would be right back. He did as he was told and chose the small wicker couch. Since his grandmother's tone was usually more polite, he could tell she was quite upset.

Rosie came back with a big scrapbook. She placed it carefully on his lap and sat down next to him on the couch. As he opened to the first page, Peter realized this was his mother's life. He kept turning the pages and saw her smiling in photos with her friends growing up, participating in school plays, parades, and even working in the library. The last page was her high school graduation.

He turned and looked up at his grandmother with a tear in his eye. "She left the next day for the city," Rosie said stoically.

"Why are you showing this to me?" he asked, not sure how this related to what had happened earlier in the evening.

"Before your mother left, she had a lifetime of love and laughter in this little town. There is something about this place. Those who stay here, do it because they love it. Those who move here, find that they'd never want to live anywhere else," she explained. "Your mother loved it here, once upon a time, until she moved to the city and met your father. She found a different kind of excitement in the city. Ramona wasn't interested in raising a family in Hope Springs like your Uncle Robert was, and that's okay. But I also don't think she'd agree with your decision to destroy it."

"She and my father did their best raising me," Peter said quietly. "I didn't have a bad childhood." He somehow felt the need to defend his parents' decision to live in the city.

Rosie smiled. "I didn't say your childhood was bad, just different. Hope Springs isn't about the excitement of the city. It's about the peace and tranquility and pride in the history and heritage. That wasn't for Ramona, and that's okay too. But it is for so many others who move here and call Hope Springs their home." She paused for a moment. "If you tear down the four buildings that were literally the cornerstone of our town, then you have lost all that Hope Springs stands for."

Peter thought for a minute. How could he tell her about his plan until he knew if it was going to work? "Grandmother, do you trust me?" he asked, taking her hand.

"I'd like to, Peter," she answered, squeezing his hand. She hated to see to people she loved dearly, hurting.

"Then trust that I have a plan that will not involve tearing anything down. Cassia went behind my back on this whole thing. She has been lying, even to me, almost from the start, and meeting

209

secretly with the mayor," he began to explain. "In fact, I haven't even met the man yet. I've asked a few people in my company that I can trust to come up with an alternative, and I should be ready to reveal it in a few days. That was why I had asked Cassia to set up a meeting with the mayor for next Friday, because then I would have the new plan ready."

"Well, why did she feel the need to ruin my birthday party?" Rosie asked, almost shouting.

Peter shook his head. "I don't think it had anything to do with you. Cassia has been trying to turn her and me into a couple for a while now. Last week when Chandler came to the city to go to the ballgame, we ran into Cassia as she was coming out of the elevator in my condo building. I told each the other was an old friend," he said. "I guess Cassia figured out Chandler was the woman who owned the bakery. My guess is that she also figured out we were dating and got jealous."

"Wow, she's a bit of a witch, isn't she?" Rosie said, shaking her head. "Of course, you shouldn't be telling fibs either, young man," she said with a raised eyebrow.

"I know, I know," Peter said, rubbing his free hand over his face. "I really do have a plan that would work. Unfortunately, I've probably lost Chandler in the process."

"Ah, Chandler," Rosie said wistfully. "That poor child has been through a lot. My advice to you would be to do whatever you can to make this right, and quickly, and then beg her for forgiveness. I know she cares deeply for you and that might just be enough."

Peter patted her hand. "Thanks for the advice, Grandmother. I'm not giving up." He just hoped his grandmother was right.

Peter left Rosie's a short time later. It was then that he realized his car was still parked at Chandler's house. *Well,* he thought, *I have to go get it.* He decided to take a detour and walk down by the Cotton Mill. As he walked past the darkened building, he thought he could hear a loud scream coming from within. Remembering Chandler's story about the jealous husband throwing his wife's lover into the thrashing machine in the mill, a shiver went through him. *Okay,* he thought, *I'm sure that was probably just a cat.* He sure hoped so, because it might be hard to sell condos that were haunted!

He continued on until he came upon the lake. As he stared out at the water, his mind must have been playing tricks on him again. He could have sworn he just saw a woman and a man holding hands, walking across the lake. *Isn't that the other part of this story,* he thought. Chandler had mentioned something about a couple holding hands walking by the lake. But just as quickly as they appeared they were gone. Peter gave his head a shake. *I need to go home and go to bed,* he thought.

Picking up the pace a little, he headed down a side street he remembered would take him to Chandler's house. As he approached her house, he saw it was completely dark, except for a light on in the living room. As much as he wanted to see her and try to explain, he knew she most likely wouldn't listen to anything he had to say. He got in his car and drove away.

Chapter 35

Chandler returned home and saw Peter's car was still in her driveway. *Great!* She thought. *Maybe if I pretend I'm not here, he'll just get in his car and drive away.* She entered the house and turned off all but one living room light, sitting in relative darkness. She had never been so humiliated in her entire life. She should have known Peter was too good to be true. He was just like all the rest; not to be trusted.

Chandler got up and walked into her bathroom. Turning on the light, she looked in the mirror and burst into tears. How had this happened? She knew she should have gone with her first instinct and not trusted Peter Frederick. But she'd listened to Rosie, MaryAnn, Myrtle and all the others tell her what a great guy he was. Aside from Rosie and MaryAnn, no one else knew who he was so why did she listen to them?

Chandler heard the knocking on her door and just wanted it to go away. She couldn't believe Peter would betray her this way. All that talk about having his engineer fix her floor, and he knew he was going to be tearing the building down anyway. She just couldn't wrap her mind around it.

The knocking grew more insistent as she continued to ignore it. She didn't want to answer it, because she feared it was Peter. She just couldn't hear his lies and excuses right then. He'd lied to her about who that woman was, telling her Cassia was an old flame. Clearly there was more to it than that.

Chandler also certainly didn't want to see Myrtle. She was so embarrassed. But despite her attempts to cover her ears, whoever was out there wasn't taking 'no' for an answer. The knocking grew to an incessant pounding, kind of like the pounding in her head.

Obviously, whoever was on the other side of the door wasn't going away.

"Chandler, it's me, Macy!" Macy nearly shouted through the door. "I brought wine."

Chandler couldn't help but crack a small smile. She grabbed the box of tissues and walked out into the living room. Chandler opened the door to find Macy holding a bottle of Merlot and two glasses.

Chandler stepped aside for Macy to enter. "You're such a good friend," she said with a small smile. "I was just glad you weren't Peter or Myrtle."

They walked to the kitchen so Chandler could pop the cork and pour them each a glass. "To all the men we've loved and hated," she said, miserably, as they raised their glasses in toast.

"Oh, Chandler, I'm so sorry," Macy said, hugging her. "I really thought Peter was different."

Chandler just started crying. "I can't believe he's going to tear down half the town! He actually stood there that first night and lied to his own grandmother! Just goes to show how men will do anything and hurt anyone for money."

Macy grabbed the bottle and went back into the living room. Chandler followed and plopped herself down on the couch in a huff. "This is so stupid," Chandler said through her tears.

"What is?" asked Macy, sitting in the loveseat. She kicked off her heels and put her feet under her.

"I've only known him for a couple of months and we've only had two dates," Chandler said. "How can this hurt this much?" She was angry at herself for hurting this way.

"Sounds to me that there is a little more than just 'like' involved here. Do you think you could possibly be in love with Peter?" Macy asked, swirling her wine in her glass.

Chandler blew her nose and thought about that. Could you really be in love with someone after just two dates? According to MaryAnn, there was no rule book and you would just know. "Oh, God, isn't this crazy? I think I'm in love with Peter!" Chandler groaned, "And now I don't ever want to see him again!"

"Well, how about if you give it a little time," Macy advised. "Maybe things will have a way of working out for the best."

"Oh, Macy," Chandler said through tears, "ever the optimist."

As they sat on the couch, Macy refilled their glasses. Having been through this kind of disappointment in her own life, she knew that Chandler needed time to think things through. It gave her a minute to decide how much she wanted to reveal to Chandler about her own past.

"I'm a realist when it comes to my own love life," Macy said, "but I'd like to think maybe your love life will turn out better."

Chandler looked at her quizzically. "Just what exactly did happen before you came to Hope Springs?" Chandler knew it was something about a bad relationship, but Macy never said anything other than that.

"Well," Macy started, "I was working for a doctor in the city, and let's just say I was young and naïve and he was married."

"Oh," Chandler whispered.

"Yeah," Macy replied, "and I didn't know that until he broke it off. That was when I heard about Dr. Howard looking for a nurse. I figured that since he was old, there'd be no chance of a repeat, and I really needed a change of scenery."

"Well, I'm so sorry that had to happen, but I'm so happy you chose to move here," Chandler acknowledged. "I honestly don't know what I'd do without you."

Chapter 36

After Macy had left Saturday night, Chandler had a restless night's sleep. She kept replaying in her mind her entire relationship with Peter, wondering if there were warning signs she had missed. There was the conversation she had overheard at the grocery store, but those ladies didn't mention Peter. Yes, Cassia had literally run into her at Peter's condo, but Peter had said she was an old girlfriend, so Chandler figured she lived in the building. Peter never let on that his company was in charge.

So, Chandler got up Sunday morning and just couldn't bring herself to go to church. She had left the party before anyone could even speak to her, and didn't know what she'd say to Rosie the next time she saw her. Rosie was so happy that she and Peter were in a relationship, and Chandler wanted to cry all over again at the thought that she'd disappointed Rosie on her birthday.

So, Chandler skipped church and instead spent the day cleaning her house from top to bottom. She knew she'd just spruced it up a few days earlier before Peter came for dinner, but it had been awhile since she'd had the time for a proper cleaning.

At one point, Chandler looked at her cell phone and saw that she had several missed calls from Myrtle, Fran, and Andrea, all leaving messages to call if she needed anything. She tried not to be disappointed that Peter wasn't among those missed calls. Macy and Hillary had texted to say they were available anytime to talk as well. She did text them both to thank them and let them know she was doing okay.

By the end of the day, everything was clean and all the laundry was done and Chandler realized that she hadn't eaten anything all day. She just didn't have the stomach for food, but knew she should eat something. She found some leftovers in her freezer and heated them in the microwave. She didn't want to go out anywhere or see anyone.

On Monday morning, Myrtle had stopped by before she left for work to see if she needed anything. She was a little surprised that Chandler actually answered the door. "Hello, honey," Myrtle said sympathetically, and she came into the house.

Chandler hugged her, surprised that she wanted to cry. "Hi, Myrtle. Can I get you anything?" she asked, leading the way back to the kitchen. "I was just getting ready to make a pot of tea."

"A pot of tea?" Myrtle asked. "Chandler, the only time you have tea is when you're sick. Do you need me to take care of you?" Myrtle wanted so much to say 'like your mother would do', but knew that would just make Chandler feel even worse. She knew that when a woman felt this bad over a man, she wanted her mother's love more than anything.

Chandler gave her a forced smile. "I'm okay, really. I just felt like tea this morning." She knew it was a weak statement, but that was all she had. She filled her tea kettle with water and put it on to boil.

"Chandler, it's going to be okay," Myrtle tried comforting her.

Chandler looked at her sideways as she took a tea bag out of the box and put it in her mug. "Please don't try and tell me there are other fish in the sea or something like that. Peter was the one man I really thought I could trust, and look where that got me."

Myrtle held up her hand, "I wasn't going to say that. I was going to say that things aren't always what they seem; a totally different overused saying," she finished, smiling.

Chandler cracked a small smile. "Myrtle, how is it that you always know what to say to make me feel a little bit better?"

Myrtle shrugged her shoulders, "It's a gift." She went over to the stove and took the hot kettle off. "Now sit down, and I'll make your tea and get you some cinnamon toast."

Chandler sat at her kitchen table and began to cry. "Just like my mom used to make?"

Myrtle smiled and walked over to hug her. "Yes, just like your mom used to make."

"Oh Myrtle, I don't know what I'd do without all of you," Chandler said between wiping tears and blowing her nose. "I miss my mom and grandma so much, but I thank God every day for you and Rosie."

Myrtle surprised herself by having to hold back the tears. She was the strong one in the group, and never let anyone see her cry. She turned to begin making the cinnamon toast. "We're here anytime you need us," she got out without getting choked up. She picked up the plate of toast and cup of tea and set them in front of Chandler. "Now eat this and get ready for work. I can see myself out, and I'll stop by the bakery to let Gretchen know you'll be a little late. I'll text Luann and tell her to get her butt in gear and go in early."

Chandler took a bite of toast and sip of tea. "Just like mom's," she said. "You know Myrtle, I never knew you had such a soft side."

"And if you ever tell anyone, I'll deny every word," Myrtle answered with a wink. "Now eat!" she ordered, as she walked down the hall and out the front door.

Chandler had made it to the bakery about an hour later than normal. She figured Myrtle must have laid down the law to Luann and Gretchen, because neither of them brought up the subject of her and Peter. They did, however, order her to stay in the back and work on cake orders all day. She figured that way she wouldn't have to deal with questions from nosey customers.

The bakery was so busy all day that she didn't have time to dwell on the fact that she may not have it much longer. By Monday night, however, she finally gave in and cried for over two hours; probably sadder about losing the bakery than losing Peter. Chandler had worked so hard for her business and couldn't believe it may all be gone soon. She had no idea what she was going to do. She finally crawled into bed and cried herself to sleep.

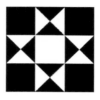

Chapter 37

Monday morning Peter skipped the gym and went straight to the office. He had called Lance and Chuck and told them to meet him at 7:00 a.m., and to bring everything they had on the new plans for Hope Springs. He hadn't heard anything from Cassia since the fiasco Saturday night, but figured she'd be making an appearance sometime that morning. He was sure she wasn't going to be happy once he was done with her.

Lance and Chuck showed up right on time. He invited them in and closed the door behind them. "Okay, gentlemen, as I explained on the phone yesterday, we need to have this proposal done by the end of today." He wasn't going to waste any more time. "So, what do you have?"

Lance rolled out the new plans he had been working on since their last meeting. He showed Peter and Chuck that it would be completely doable to build a new structure in the space behind the police station. "There is also room on the other side of the street behind the Hilltop Restaurant," Lance explained, "and that building could use the parking lot behind the bank. I would recommend we do two buildings that are the same height as the existing structures, so they don't stand out."

"I like where you are going with this, Lance," Peter agreed. "Get me what I need to present this to the mayor by tomorrow. Also, be sure to include an estimate on revamping the park." Peter turned to Chuck. "What I need from you is an estimate on what needs to be done to revive the existing structures. I don't want to take away the character, just spruce them up and make any improvements for safety."

"Sure thing," Chuck nodded. "I can have that for you tomorrow as well."

"Good work, men," Peter said, walking toward the door. "I think this new plan is really going to make a lot of people happy."

As Lance and Chuck left, all Peter cared about was that it made one person in particular happy. He had spent the better part of Sunday kicking himself for not being completely honest with Chandler. She had told him she'd been lied to in her previous relationship and that was the reason she broke it off. It had taken every ounce of self-control he had not to call her, but he knew he needed to give her time and he wanted to figure out his new plan first.

Once Pat came in, he asked her to schedule a dinner meeting with the mayor of Hope Springs for the following night. "Make it at the Hilltop Restaurant and ask for one of their small private dining rooms." With that finished, he picked up the phone and called his Aunt MaryAnn.

"Hello, Peter," answered MaryAnn, more cheerfully than he had expected. "What can I do for you this morning?"

"First off, thanks for answering the phone even though you knew it was me," he said, glad she was still speaking to him.

"Peter, what happened Saturday night was not your fault," MaryAnn said. "I hope, however, you're calling to tell me you have some kind of grand plan to fix this mess."

"As a matter of fact I do, and I need your help," he said with a smile. Peter went on to explain that he would also need the help of the Advice Quilting Bee. "Do you think they would help?" he asked hesitantly.

"If Rosie says she needs their help, they will," MaryAnn said. "I like this plan, Peter. Is that all you need?"

"Actually, I'm going to be meeting with the mayor tomorrow night at the Hilltop, and need to make sure Chandler doesn't see us together," he explained. "Is there any way you can get her out of town for the evening?"

"As a matter of fact, there is," MaryAnn chuckled. "A new winery just opened up and a few of us have wanted to go. It's about twenty minutes outside of town, so that would be perfect. I'll invite Chandler and insist she go along."

"You're the best, Aunt MaryAnn," Peter said, grateful to know she was behind him. "The tab will be on me. Give me the name of the winery and I'll call them with my credit card number."

"I like the sound of that!" exclaimed MaryAnn. "Now you just do your part and fix this!"

"Yes, ma'am, I intend to," he told her, silently praying his plan would work. It had to because he had no other options.

MaryAnn gave Peter the name of the winery, and he said he'd take care of the rest. After they said their goodbyes, Peter hung up feeling even more confident in his plan.

With everything falling into place, Peter was finally starting to calm, until Cassia barged in.

"Peter Frederick!" she shouted, hands on her hips. "Just what kind of people live in that little village anyway?"

Peter could swear her skirt was a few inches shorter. "Just what little village are you referring to?"

"Oh, don't play games with me!" she shouted, brushing her long blonde hair from her eyes. "That God-forsaken place called Hope Springs."

"Watch it, my family lives in Hope Springs," Peter said, defensively. Then he remembered seeing Myrtle and Fran near Cassia's car on Saturday night. "Why, did something happen?" he asked, innocently, trying not to smile.

"Ugh, yes, something happened!" she practically shouted. "Somehow I managed to get two flat tires. Then, it took forever and cost me a small fortune to get my car towed back to the city. I had to call a private driver, because there are no taxis in that Godforsaken place. I'm expensing all of it!"

Peter would gladly pay the bill on this one. He was laughing on the inside, but wasn't about to let her know it. *God bless the Little Old Lady Network*, he thought.

"Since you brought up Saturday night," he said sternly, "I'm not sure just what you were trying to accomplish with that stunt, but you've managed to get yourself fired."

Cassia actually had the nerve to look shocked. "Fired?!" she shouted.

Peter noticed that Pat had silently shut the door. "Yes, fired!" he shouted back. "You completely went behind my back and undermined my authority at every turn with the Hope Springs Project. I can't trust you. And if I can't trust you, you have no place here at Frederick Development, Inc."

"I've put my heart and soul into that project! I, I mean, *we* stand to make a lot of money, all because of me!" She stomped her foot like a two-year-old, for emphasis.

"Just how much of a kickback are you getting," he asked to see if she'd bite.

"How dare you accuse me of such a thing!" she screamed, having the audacity of looking shocked at his suggestion.

"That's fine Cassia, you don't need to reveal your profits to me. Maybe you'll reveal them to my lawyers when I sue you. This isn't the first time you have mentioned 'you, I mean we,' making money on this deal." He knew it would be easy enough to find out if she really stood to profit personally if the deal went through.

"Lawyers?" she cried. "Do we really need to bring lawyers into this?"

Peter sat back in his chair and put his feet up on the desk. "Well, I could be persuaded not to sue you, if you just go quietly into the night. If, however, you choose to put up a fuss, then you better get an attorney," he said, with a smug expression.

She actually started crying, "But Peter, I did all of this for us. I don't understand what you see in that baker anyway. I'm so much more sophisticated than she is. She could never fit into your world, and do you really think you could move to that little rundown village for the rest of your life?" she cried, mascara running down her face.

"Yes, I do," he said very confidently. Putting his feet on the floor and sitting up, he asked "So, what's it going to be? Am I calling my lawyers, or am I never going to hear from you again?"

She snarled at him defiantly, all traces of tears long gone. "I'll be out of my office by the end of the day."

As she started to storm out of the office, Peter called for Pat to come in. "Pat, Ms. Collins will no longer be employed by Frederick Development, Inc., as of 4:00 this afternoon. Would you please take care of the necessary paperwork? Oh, and please arrange for security to escort her out once she has packed her things." After seeing the shocked expression on Cassia's face he added, "And make sure she doesn't take anything that doesn't belong to her."

Peter could see Pat was smiling from ear to ear, but discreetly hiding her expression behind a file folder she was holding. "Of course, I'll take care of everything." She turned to Cassia. "Right this way," Pat said politely, as she waved her hand for Cassia to go out the door in front of her.

Cassia held her head high and began to walk out of Peter's office. Before she could get to the door, he said, "Oh, and one more thing."

"What?" Cassia asked, with sinking shoulders.

"You were wrong."

"About what?" she asked dejectedly.
"Hope Springs is a town, not a village," Peter corrected with a big smile.

Cassia stomped her foot one more time, slamming the door for good measure.

Chapter 38

Monday night, Peter walked into the lobby of his condo feeling like a new man. His plans were coming along and he hoped that by the end of the week, he and Chandler would be back together.

"Good evening, Mr. Frederick," Carl said, as he entered. "You certainly look better this evening than you did Saturday night. I take it everything is alright?"

"Hello, Carl," Peter said with a smile. "Yes, today was definitely a productive day. If the rest of the week goes as planned, I may be putting my condo on the market and moving to the country."

"Wow, that's quite a leap," Carl replied, with raised eyebrows. "Guess that means everything is going well with your lady friend?"

"Well," Peter hesitated. He knew he could count on Carl to be discreet, and actually he really wanted his take on everything that had happened. "Here is what happened in a nutshell. I wasn't totally honest with Chandler about my business."

"So, you lied to her," Carl stated, slowly shaking his head from side to side.

"Yes, I lied," Peter said. He could say he omitted the truth, but he knew what he had done and was man enough to admit it. "Things were going really well personally, but what I didn't realize was that Cassia—you remember her?" Carl shook his head in the affirmative. "Well, she decided to crash my grandmother's birthday party to announce to the whole town that my company was going to demolish four very historic buildings to build new offices. One of those happened to be the building Chandler rents for her bakery."

"Oh," Carl remarked, with empathy, "I'm sure that didn't go over well."

Peter rubbed his hands over his face. "No, it didn't. But what everyone, including Cassia, didn't realize was that I was already working on a different proposal to save the buildings and build somewhere else in town. Unfortunately, my plans weren't ready to present yet, so Chandler never had the chance to hear that part of the story."

"And when will she?" Carl asked.

"That's what I've been working on all day today. I'm meeting with the mayor of Hope Springs tomorrow to present my proposal and to let him know that this is the only option from my company," he explained. "If that flies, then I'll be telling Chandler on Thursday night, with the help of her friends in the Advice Quilting Bee."

"That all sounds promising, but what is the Advice Quilting Bee?" Carl asked, curiously.

"A group of ladies my grandmother put together. They make quilts for very deserving causes and apparently also give each other advice on their own lives," Peter explained. "I'm just hoping they aren't going to advise Chandler not to give me a second chance."

"I see," Carl said, understanding. "So, what happened to Cassia?" he asked, curious to hear how this turned out.

"I fired her this morning for going behind my back," Peter answered with a big smile.

"Wow, you have had a busy day, Mr. Frederick!" Carl said with a laugh.

"Yes, Carl, I have, and I still have more to do to get ready for my meeting with the mayor tomorrow, so I'd better get upstairs and get busy."

"I'll say a little prayer for you tonight that everything works out for you," Carl said with a smile.

"Thanks, I'm going to need all the help I can get," Peter replied with a wry grin.

As Peter got on the elevator, he thought about what he had just said to Carl. The idea of moving from this cold building into a smaller home that was more of a home sounded better and better. He could just as easily run his business from there as he could from his office here. Being able to spend more time with family was worth everything, he just hoped that family included Chandler.

When Peter entered his condo, he took a good look around. He wanted to see his place through Chandler's eyes. He realized he had no pictures of himself, or any member of his family for that matter. He had no memorabilia from his past; nothing to show what he'd been like as a boy.

Where had all that stuff gone? He thought. Peter wondered if it was still at his parents' house. Maybe it was time for him to mend that fence as well. He looked at his watch and saw that it was still early, so he dialed the number he knew by heart and waited for the familiar voice to answer.

"Hi, dad," Peter hoped his father wouldn't hang up on him.

"Well, hello, Peter," James Frederick answered. "It's been a long time, son." He wondered what precipitated this call from Peter.

Peter winced at the reference his father made to the length of time since they'd last spoken. "I know," he acknowledged, "and I'm sorry I haven't called sooner." He didn't want to bring up the fact that his father hadn't tried to call him either. This call wasn't about placing blame, it was about calling a truce. "Dad, if you're going to be around tomorrow, I'd like to get together for lunch. I could come over to the house around noon if that works for you."

"I'd like that very much," James answered. There were things James needed to talk to Peter about, but he just couldn't bring himself to make the call. "I'm glad you called, son," he added.

Peter smiled. "Me too, dad. I'll see you tomorrow." And before he hung up, he added, "Dad, I love you." He thought he heard his dad say 'I love you' back, but couldn't be sure. He smiled again, glad that he'd made the call.

Chapter 39

"Good morning, ladies! Something sure smells good in here," MaryAnn said, as she entered the bakery on Tuesday. "I could smell the cinnamon rolls and chocolate muffins all the way from Rosie's." After her conversation with Peter the previous day, MaryAnn had spent the better part of the afternoon coming up with a plan to get Chandler out of town for the evening. She was here to implement said plan.

"Hi there, MaryAnn," Gretchen yelled from the back of the bakery. "If you're looking for Chandler, she is running a little slow this morning."

"Good, I wanted to talk to you before she got here," MaryAnn answered as she came to the back. "How was she yesterday?" MaryAnn had purposely stayed away from the bakery, because she didn't want to slip and say something about Peter's plan.

"Oh, she wasn't as bubbly as she had been last week, if that's what you're asking." Gretchen was putting the finishing touches on a tray of cinnamon. "We were out of town over the weekend and missed Rosie's birthday bash. From what I could gather from Chandler, it didn't go well. Just what happened, anyway?"

MaryAnn eyed the gooey cinnamon rolls. "Honestly, I'd weigh 300 pounds if I worked here," she sighed. She went on to explain the whole sordid mess. "God bless Peter, he has a plan that we are hoping is going to work. It would save everything, including their relationship." At least she hoped it would.

"That's good, because the Chandler that was here yesterday was a bear to work for," Gretchen replied, moving the tray to the display case before beginning work on a batch of cookies.

"So, what I need from you," MaryAnn continued, "is to make sure I can take Chandler out of here by 5:00 this evening. A few of us are taking her to a winery about twenty minutes outside of town."

"That will be no problem," Gretchen said. "We don't have any orders for tomorrow, and Luann is coming in today. There won't be any reason for her to stay late."

"Great!" MaryAnn smiled. The door opened and Chandler walked in, looking more dejected than MaryAnn had ever seen her. Even when she and Victor had broken up, she didn't look this bad.

"Hello, dear," MaryAnn said, hugging her.

"Hi," Chandler said, glumly. "Are you here to check up on me?"
"Of course not," MaryAnn replied, smiling. "I'm here to invite you to join me and a few of your friends for drinks at a new winery that just opened up. Tonight is Ladies Night."

"Oh, I'm not really in the mood to be around a bunch of people, especially not a Ladies Night. You know the place will be crawling with single men," Chandler said quietly.

"That's the beauty of *this* Ladies Night," answered MaryAnn excitedly. "No men allowed!"

"Sounds like just what you need," Gretchen yelled from the back as she put two large trays of cookies in the oven.

Chandler looked between them, fighting the desire to crawl back into bed with the glimmer of excitement she felt over getting out of town for an evening. She knew they were only trying to help, and maybe a night out with the girls was just what she needed. "Okay, I'll go," she said, reluctantly.

"Wonderful!" shouted MaryAnn. "I'll pick you up at your place tonight at 5:45. That should give you enough time to go home and freshen up." *And maybe put on some make-up*, she added silently.

"Yes, that should be fine," answered Chandler, trying for a smile that never quite reached her face. MaryAnn noticed her emerald green eyes seemed to have lost some of their sparkle.

"Gretchen, can I have one of those delicious cinnamon rolls and a cup of coffee to go?" MaryAnn asked. "I just don't have the willpower to fight it."

Gretchen filled her order, and Chandler told her it was on the house. "You can buy my first glass of wine tonight."

"Sounds like a plan," MaryAnn said, giving Chandler a hug. "See you tonight."

Chandler watched MaryAnn walk out the door. She was so glad she had such great friends. They were always there when she needed them.

Chapter 40

Peter took a deep breath and used the brass lion-head door knocker to announce his arrival. As he stood in front of the oversized wooden door waiting for it to open, he once again went over in his mind the last time he'd been there.

He and his father had just returned from his mother's funeral. As they sat in the study, Peter waited for his father to say something, anything. But the older gentleman just sat looking out the window. Beyond him, Peter could see the ocean; the waves building and crashing at the shoreline, much like he was sure his father felt like his life had come crashing in.

Peter and his father never really had the typical father-son relationship. His father's life revolved around two things – work and Peter's mother. He had retired early, and was looking forward to spending the rest of his life spoiling Peter's mother with trips and lavish gifts. And then that dream was gone.

Peter knew he should have been grieving like his father, but to be honest, he really didn't know his mother any more than he knew his father. They had all lived in this enormous house, but he had his life and they had theirs. Sometimes their paths would cross at the dinner table, but more often than not, he would be eating with the housekeeper, Victoria. What a sad life, he thought to himself. But he was here to make amends with his family, because Chandler had shown him the importance of family in one's life.

The big door opening brought Peter back to the present and he saw the housekeeper he'd grown so fond of. "Hello, Victoria," Peter said, smiling. "Long time, no see."

"Oh, Peter!" Victoria cried out loud, throwing her arms around him. It felt good to know someone in his house was happy to see him. "Come in, come in," she said, ushering Peter into the vast entryway. She looked him up and down. "You're looking good."

"You're looking pretty terrific yourself," Peter told her. Man, he'd missed Victoria's smile.

"Your father said you were coming for lunch," Victoria told him as she closed the massive door behind him. "Come on into the kitchen and let me get you some lemonade," she said, leading him down the hallway.

"You always made the best lemonade," Peter complimented her. As they walked down the long entry hall to the back of the house, which was really a mansion, Peter thought about Chandler's home. He could go from the front door to the back door of her cottage in about ten steps, while this walk seemed more like thirty steps. And where Chandler's home had warm cream-colored walls and hardwood flooring, his parents' home was full of cold marble and granite tile.

As they reached the kitchen, Victoria interrupted his thoughts to ask, "So what finally made you decide to come and see your father?" Victoria was nothing if not direct.

Peter watched her retrieve a cut-glass pitcher of fresh lemonade from the oversize refrigerator. As she got a glass from the cabinet and filled it with ice, she gave him a look over her shoulder meant to say, 'I'm waiting'.

Peter suddenly had a flashback to another time he'd been sitting at this same counter waiting for Victoria to pour him a glass of lemonade. He'd gotten into trouble in high school, and Victoria had given him that same look waiting for him to explain his actions. He shook the thought off and answered. "I've met someone." There, bring on the twenty questions.

"And?" was all she said.

What? Peter thought. *I've come all the way out here and told you I've met someone, and that's all you can say?* "And, I thought what was left of my family should know. Grandmother Rosie knows, but I thought I should tell my father."

Slowly, a smile spread across Victoria's face. "You have to understand that there have been many women in your life, Peter. How is this one different?"

Peter couldn't argue with her there. "Well, if I can get her to trust me again, this is the last one."

"You've messed up," Victoria said, more of a statement than a question.

"Yes, I messed up," Peter said, taking a long sip of lemonade. "But I have a plan to make it right. I just hope Chandler will forgive me." He knew there were no guarantees that would happen.

"And you are here to ask your father for help?" Victoria asked, leaning against the counter much the same as she'd had so many times before when Peter needed to confide in someone and his parents weren't home.

Peter shook his head. "No, I have that all taken care of. I'm here to see dad because Chandler has shown me how important family is." When he could tell Victoria wasn't following, he continued. "Chandler Bradford is her name. Her parents and grandparents have all passed away. All she has are the women of the Advice Quilting Bee. They are her family now."

"What is the Advice Quilting Bee?" Victoria asked, beginning to understand where Peter was going.

"A group of women in Hope Springs who really look out for each other," Peter answered. "But that's not important. The important thing is that I'm here to try and patch things up with dad."

Victoria clapped her hands, "whatever the reason, I'm just glad you're finally here. I think your father is in his study."

Peter finished his drink and put the glass on the sparkling granite counter. "Before I go see him, do you know what happened to all my stuff from high school and college?"

Victoria gave him an odd look, "it's still in your old room." She should know, because she was the one who went in there every week to dust all the trophies, ribbons, and other memorabilia he'd collected over the years.

"Really?" Peter asked, surprised his mother hadn't cleaned it all out to make another guest room. The house had extra guest rooms already, but she had always been entertaining. Peter couldn't remember a weekend when they didn't have houseguests.

"Peter," Victoria began, softly, "your parents made sure it was exactly the way it was when you left. Your mother, especially, wanted to make sure everything was ready for you if and when you decided to come for it."

That surprised Peter even more. His parents never were much for coming to his games and cheering him on. In fact, he couldn't remember ever seeing them at a single event. Peter turned and quickly made his way up the back staircase to the second floor and down the hall to his room. He opened the door and couldn't believe his eyes.

"Oh my," Peter sighed as he looked around his childhood bedroom. Nothing had changed, and yet, something was different. He still had all the ribbons from swimming and track, and trophies from football, basketball, and baseball. But looking closer, Peter also saw photographs. Action shots. Of him. "Who in the world took these?" Peter asked out loud.

"I did," came a familiar voice behind him.

Chapter 41

"Hello, dad," Peter said, turning to see his father for the first time since his mother's funeral. He reached out to shake his father's hand.

James Frederick looked from his son's hand to his face. He figured he should have expected the formality, but it still hurt. He reached out and shook Peter's hand. "How have you been, son?"

"Good," Peter answered, "and you?" *Good grief,* Peter thought, *we sound more like acquaintances than father and son.*

Peter removed his hand and turned back to the photos scattered about the room. "You took *all* these?" he asked picking up one of him playing football. "This was when I caught the ball for the winning touchdown in the championship game!" Peter couldn't believe all this. "I never even knew you were there," he said, sounding disappointed.

James walked into the room and went over to pick up a photo of Peter hitting a game-winning home run. "I didn't want to make you nervous."

What? "I didn't think you cared. All these years, I thought you didn't care!" Peter was almost shaking. He had never seen either of his parents invest any time in his life. They were always busy working or going out with their friends. Or so he thought.

James wasn't sure what to say. "We were so proud of you, Peter," he said quietly.

"We?" Peter asked, incredulous. "You mean mom was there too?" How could he have not seen them at his events?

"We would be way up in the stands so we wouldn't be a distraction," James explained. "Your mom couldn't stand listening to people yell at you for dropping a pass, or striking out. So, a lot of times we sat on the away side."

"Really?" Peter asked, shocked by what he was hearing. "I can understand your not wanting to make me nervous," Peter remembered both his parents being perfectionists and preaching to him that he had to be the best at everything, "but do you know that I would have given anything to look up into the stands and see my parents like all the other boys did?" *What a shame,* Peter thought.

Peter turned his back to his father and looked out his bedroom window. Beyond the pool and expansive, perfectly manicured lawn, the waves were once again crashing against the seawall. Peter now had a taste of what his father must have felt the day of his mother's funeral. His emotions were all over the place, and crashing into the proverbial seawall.

James reached up and put a hand on his son's shoulder. "We may not have been able to show it, son, but your mother and I loved you more than anything. And we're so proud of the man you've become."

Peter turned and threw his arms around his father. He may not have had the most outwardly loving parents growing up, but at least now he knew they did, in fact, love him. He could feel his dad embrace him in return. "I love you, dad," Peter whispered.

"I love you too, son," James said, choking up.

"I hate to break up this father-son bonding moment" Victoria interrupted, "but lunch is almost ready. I'll serve it on the back patio." She turned and walked back down the hall, sending a silent prayer to whomever orchestrated this long-overdue reunion.

James broke the hug first. "Well, I guess we better head downstairs."

"Dad, before we go," Peter began, "would it be okay if I took some of these things to my place?"

"Sure, son," James answered. "These are your things. We've just kept them dusted, or at least Victoria has, until you were ready to embrace your past. I know that when you moved into your condo, though, you had mentioned this stuff wouldn't really fit your décor. Why the change?"

Peter smiled. "I'll tell you all about her at lunch, but I've met someone who has shown me how important family and memories are in a person's life."

"Is this the young baker in Hope Springs?" James asked with a smile.

Peter looked at his father with a shocked expression. "How do you know about Chandler?" He knew Rosie hadn't said anything.

"Cassia Collins' father and I play golf together," James shrugged. "For what it's worth, I'd have fired her too."

"Yea, well, in the process I've made a mess of things," Peter said, frustratedly running his fingers through his hair. "But I have a plan to make things right and I hope it works."

"I'm sure whatever you've come up with will do the trick," James told his son. "Just follow your instincts and your heart." He patted his son on the back. "Now we'd better get downstairs or Victoria is going to be mad at both of us."

As they walked into the kitchen, Peter watched as his father walked over and gave Victoria a kiss on the cheek. "Honey, Peter wants to take some of his stuff with him."

"Hallelujah!" Victoria cheered. "I'm tired of dusting all that stuff." She put her arms around Peter's father.

Honey? "Wait a minute," Peter put a hand up, "Are you two?" he wasn't even sure what to ask.

Victoria held up her hand, "We're engaged!"

James got a concerned look on his face, "You don't mind, do you son?"

"Mind?" Peter asked, a little shocked. "Heavens no, I'm thrilled for you both!"

"We haven't set a date yet," James told him. "But when we do, you'll be the first to know."

"Alright then," Peter replied, smiling, "but for now, I'm starving."

"Lead the way, dear," James motioned for Victoria to head out to the patio.

As they sat having lunch, they talked about their plans, and Peter filled them in on Chandler. He couldn't believe how much his life had changed in such a short time. Now, if he could get Chandler to forgive him, everything would be perfect!

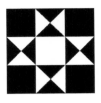

Chapter 42

"Okay, ladies," Rosie began as the members of the Advice Quilting Bee held a special session on Tuesday evening, "I want to thank all of you for taking time out of your week to help with this special project, but please remember, this is top secret." Before his meeting with the mayor, Peter had dropped off a copy of the plan for Rosie and her team to work their magic.

Myrtle looked around the room at the assembled group. Aside from MaryAnn, Hillary, and Macy, who were charged with occupying Chandler for the evening, everyone else was in attendance. *This proves just how much Chandler is loved*, she thought. "This project is different from anything we've ever done, because all of us are going to be assembling it, not just Rosie and me."

Rosie and Myrtle had already laid out the pattern for everyone to follow on one of the cutting tables. "As you can see," began Myrtle, "the finished quilt will make up our version of the town, and will be approximately thirty inches by seventy inches. Our job is to piece together representations of the structures, stores, etc. that will make up Main Street itself according to the plan Peter and his team have designed. This will also include upgrades to our park."

Fran looked at the pattern. "So, he has come up with a way that saves all the buildings and keeps Main Street in tact?"

"Yes, he has," Rosie answered, proudly. "And he believes the mayor will approve. He's presenting it to him now. I'm sure we all know the town council will as well. The new development will be on vacant lots behind existing structures so as not to disturb the small town feel we all love." When Peter had approached Rosie with the plans, she was so happy he'd found a way to use the vacant lots.

"This is such an awesome idea for a quilt," Andrea said, smiling. "I'm so glad he's including us. We all love Chandler and would do whatever it takes to see her happy again."

Candy carried a big box of fabric over to the table. "Here is all our scrap fabric we have saved from other projects. Let's all take a section of the pattern and get started."

"Exactly what would be the best way to accomplish this in such a short amount of time?" asked Fran, figuring that traditional piecing would be next to impossible.

"Well," began Rosie, "the process Myrtle and I came up with goes against everything most quilters stand for; however, desperate times call for desperate measures." She reached under the cutting table and pulled out a box of glue sticks.

"You want us to glue the quilt together?" asked Andrea, surprised.

"Yes," answered Myrtle. "This won't be a quilt in the traditional sense. More of a pieced picture. We will be gluing pieces of fabric directly onto the pattern, with no seaming involved. Our goal here is to make something Chandler will recognize as our town, only updated."

"Who knows," said Rosie, "if we do a really great job, we can frame it and hang it in the visitor's center."

"That's a great idea!" exclaimed Fran. "This could show folks there is more than one way to make a quilt. I believe this method would be called fiber art."

"Okay, get working, fiber artists," ordered Myrtle. "We have a lot to do in a very short amount of time. We need to have it done by our meeting on Thursday."

"Wow, that really isn't a lot of time," said Andrea.

Chapter 43

Peter arrived for his meeting with the mayor about fifteen minutes early and parked the company car he'd driven in the back. Aunt MaryAnn had texted him that they would be getting Chandler out of town for the evening, but he didn't want to take any chances.

The private dining room Pat had reserved was perfect. Besides being secluded, it also enabled him to spread out so everything could be viewed at the same time. He really hoped this worked. His future with Chandler depended on it.

The mayor arrived on time, and Peter introduced himself. "I believe you know my grandmother, Rosie Macintire," he added.

"Oh, yes," the mayor said, shaking Peter's hand, "I remember you when you were a little boy. Your grandmother speaks very highly of you."

"I'm quite fond of her as well," Peter said, smiling.

"I must admit," the mayor began, "I was quite surprised that I never got to deal with you. Ms. Collins informed me that it was your company, but that she would be making all the decisions and presenting the proposal."

"Well, Ms. Collins is no longer with the company," Peter stated. He also didn't want to bring up the subject of kickbacks, just in case he'd been wrong about that even though he truly didn't think he was.

The mayor just clapped his hands together and said, "My secretary says you have an alternative proposal. Let's order some dinner and you can tell me all about it."

The mayor summoned the waitress, and they each placed their dinner order. Once drinks had been delivered, Peter took the opportunity to show the mayor the new plan. During his presentation, Peter could see him nod in agreement for a lot of his suggestions. *This looks promising,* Peter thought.

"So, as you can see," Peter concluded, silently praying he'd done enough to persuade the mayor, "this could be a win-win for everyone."

The mayor took a sip of his coffee and smiled. "Mr. Frederick, I like your plan, and more importantly, I think the town council and residents will like it too. You've managed to capture the spirit of the town and still bring us into the twenty-first century. And changing the new buildings to two-story instead of four will really make them blend in nicely."

Once dinner was served, Peter decided to keep going with his ideas. "I also have another project I'd like to propose to you."

"Okay," replied the mayor, "let's hear it."

"How would you feel about taking the Cotton Mill and converting it into condos?" Peter asked. "The town owns the property and could make a profit by selling them."

"Another great idea," he said, smiling. "The building is just sitting there costing us money anyway. Might was well use it for something."

Once they had finished their meals, Peter said, "Sir, I would appreciate it if you would keep our conversation private for now. Another part of this is mending fences with some of the ladies in town whom I have hurt. I'll be taking care of that on Thursday evening, and then we can get the town council approval."

"Absolutely, young man." The mayor winked, and said, "I was young once too, you know."

Peter smiled at that.

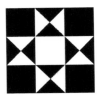

Chapter 44

As Peter was meeting with the mayor, and the ladies were beginning work on the quilt, the rest of the group was trying to cheer Chandler up at the winery. "This is a beautiful location," MaryAnn said as they were exiting the car. The winery was nestled in the valley with the Virginia mountains on either side.

"If it's this beautiful in the summer, can you imagine what it will be like in the fall," agreed Macy, referring to all the trees surrounding the property.

As they walked up the drive from the parking lot to the main building, Hillary linked arms with Chandler. "Tonight we drink to happy times," she said, smiling. "We'll only talk about topics you wish to discuss."

Chandler looked at her. "In other words, if I want to talk about my love life, we can. If I don't, we won't."

"Exactly," Hillary answered, smiling. Hillary knew a little something about bad relationships, having lived through an abusive, five-year marriage. Luckily, she'd been able to divorce him and move to Hope Springs to begin a new life. "You know, I thought my life was over after my divorce, but then I moved to Hope Springs and all that changed."

"That's right," said Chandler. "Wasn't that when you met Jack?"

"Yes," answered Hillary. "I was working at Fran's, and he came in for some ice cream. He had just gotten his CPA's license and moved here from the city. He was renting one of the apartments above Fran's. I was actually living above what is now the bakery. He was calm and very astute. He could tell I was a 'wounded bird', so he was very patient and kind," she smiled at the memory.

"How did you know he wouldn't hurt you like your ex had?" asked Chandler, feeling a little like a wounded bird herself.

"I could tell from the beginning he was nothing like my ex, but it still took a little while for me to trust him. Eventually, though, I knew he was the man for me," she said with a smile. "And the rest, as they say, is history. We took a leap of faith and bought the building between the diner and the post office. We spent a lot of time fixing it up and making the downstairs my shop and his CPA office, and the upstairs our home."

By now the group had been seated on the deck facing west, so they could watch the sunset over the mountain ridge. "And now your entire life is also slated for demolition," Chandler said sadly. "I really thought Peter was my knight in shining armor, but I guess I was wrong, and let everyone down."

The others looked at each other, wishing they could tell her what they knew, but knowing they couldn't. "What do you mean about letting everyone down?" asked MaryAnn.

"I was the one who was supposed to be checking him out and seeing if he was up to no good," Chandler said, frustrated. "Instead, I ended up falling in love with him!"

"Chandler, you can't blame yourself," said Macy, trying to calm her down. "You had no idea what he was up to!"

The waiter came and MaryAnn ordered a bottle of their finest red wine for the table, as well as an assortment of appetizers. The others just looked at her as the waiter left. "Oh, this is on me," she said, sensing they knew the amount of money this night was going to cost. They didn't know the tab was already taken care of, and she was going to make sure Peter paid a pretty penny for hurting Chandler the way he had. She also knew he would pay whatever it took to get Chandler back.

"Wow!" exclaimed Hillary. "Did Robert bring home a little extra from the bank today?"

"Something like that," MaryAnn answered, smiling. She'd fill the others in later. "Chandler, perhaps Peter didn't really mean to lie to you, but wasn't sure what to say until he had everything worked out." MaryAnn felt an obligation to defend her nephew.

"Maybe," Chandler said, watching the sun set behind the mountain. The beautiful colors of purple, pink, and orange mixed across the sky in sharp contrast to the constant gray mood she seemed to be in these days.

A different waiter appeared with their order and poured each of them a glass of red wine. "Enjoy," he said, "and please let me know if there is anything else I can get for you."

Chandler looked up at him. "Can you find me a man who won't lie to me or hurt me?"

He looked at her with a smile. "Something tells me you may have found him already, but haven't yet figured that out. Sometimes those we love the most hurt us without knowing it, because they are trying to do the right thing. Just because he didn't tell you the truth at the time, doesn't mean he did it to be mean or to consciously hurt you. In an effort to find a better solution, he may have not been totally truthful with you at that moment."

The other three looked from the waiter to each other as if wondering if he knew the whole story. MaryAnn finally noticed his name tag. Steven. "Thank you, Steven," she said. "We'll let you know if we need anything else."

After Steven walked away, Macy asked, "That wasn't the same waiter who took our order, was it?"

"No," answered MaryAnn, still processing what he had just said. "Our first waiter was much younger."

"You know," Chandler said, "my father's name was Steven, spelled the same way and everything. Strange."

As they enjoyed their very expensive bottle of wine and plates of appetizers, Chandler's mood began to improve. "Thank you all so much for bringing me here," she said with tears in her eyes. "This was just what I needed."

"I think that deserves a toast," said Hillary. They all toasted with near empty glasses.

Since they hadn't seen Steven for a while now, and they really needed to be going, MaryAnn motioned for their original waiter. "Would you please tell Steven we're ready for our check?"

"Steven?" he asked, "Ma'am, we have no waiters by that name. In fact, we have no one on the entire staff with that name."

Chandler just stared at him, "Are you serious?"

"Positive," was his reply. "Let me clear some of these plates for you and I'll bring the check."

All four just looked at each other. "Chandler, you said your father's name was Steven?" asked Macy, seeming to confirm what she had said earlier.

"Uh huh," Chandler said with a slow nod. "Please don't tell me you're all thinking what I'm thinking?"

"I think we are," Hillary acknowledged. The possibility that Chandler's late father came to deliver a message was a little bit more than any of them wanted to admit.

"Well," began MaryAnn, "I'm usually a skeptic, but I have to admit it was a bit of a coincidence."

The waiter brought the check in a small black folder and handed it to MaryAnn. She opened it so the others couldn't see the contents and saw a note, *"Compliments of Chandler's future husband, Peter. Signed, Steven Bradford"*. MaryAnn tried to keep the shocked expression from her face. "Chandler, did you ever speak to Peter about your parents?" she asked. "Did you ever mention their names?"

Chandler thought for a moment, "I told him the story of how they died, but I don't remember if I mentioned their names. Why?"

"Just wondering," MaryAnn said, thinking that maybe he could have gotten that information from any number of places. She'd have to follow up on this little mystery.

Placing the black folder on her lap, and her purse in front of her on the table, MaryAnn pretended to place money in the folder. She took the note out and stuck it in her purse, pretending it was the receipt. "Okay, ladies, I do believe it's time to head back to Hope Springs."

As they were walking out to the parking lot, they looked up at the darkened sky and saw a shooting star. Chandler smiled because she knew then that she had just received a message from her father.

Once they'd returned to Hope Springs, MaryAnn called Peter. "How did the meeting go with the mayor?" she asked.

"Great!" answered Peter, excitedly. "He loved all my ideas, so we're full steam ahead. How did the winery trip go?"

"It went well. I ordered the most expensive wine in the place and plenty of appetizers!" she exclaimed, smiling. "I think we actually cheered Chandler up a little."

"Well, I told you to do whatever it took to cheer her up, and it was on me," he said, laughing. "If you accomplished that, I'll gladly pay the bill."

"I have a question, though," MaryAnn continued. "Do you happen to know Chandler's late parents' names?"

"No, I don't remember Chandler telling me their names," he answered. "Why?"

"You had no idea her father's name was Steven Bradford?" she asked, wanting to confirm.
"No, why?" he asked curiously.

"I know this may sound strange, but I think Chandler's late father was one of our servers tonight, and also gave Chandler a good bit of advice as well," MaryAnn said.

"You know, Aunt MaryAnn, that doesn't sound as strange as you might think," Peter answered, thinking back to his experience by the lake. "As long as it's advice to take me back, I don't care who delivers it," he remarked, laughing.

"True. I'll be checking with Rosie and Myrtle tomorrow to make sure everything is on track for Thursday. You just make sure you do your part and not blow this opportunity," she cautioned him.

"Don't worry," he assured her. "I have way too much at stake to blow it now. Thanks for all your help, Aunt MaryAnn. I really appreciate it."

"I'm just a sucker for true love," MaryAnn answered. "See you Thursday night."

Peter laughed into the phone. "See you then."

Chapter 45

Chandler had spent all of Wednesday thinking about what the waiter had told her. *Maybe I can find a way to forgive Peter for lying to me,* she thought. *And was that really my father delivering a message?* She really hoped so.

By Thursday morning, Chandler was feeling like there was some big secret that she wasn't allowed in on. As she was going into the bakery, she spotted Myrtle, Fran and Mabel, heading into Rosie's. They actually looked around to see if anyone was watching them as they went in. *Why are they going to Rosie's this early in the morning?* She wondered.

Later on, the mayor, of all people, came into the bakery and looked around at the building. Chandler couldn't remember a time when he had scrutinized the structure that way. She just figured he wanted to get a good look at it before it was torn down. He stepped gingerly on the loose floor boards. "Chandler, does your landlord have a plan to fix this?" he asked. "We wouldn't want any of your customers getting hurt and suing him."

"The landlord doesn't have any intention of fixing it," she informed him. "However, I have a plan to barter with a contractor to get it fixed, but it seems pointless now that it's going to be torn down."

"I see," was all he said. He bought a couple of cinnamon rolls for the road and left.

"That was strange," Gretchen remarked from the cake decorating table. Chandler didn't know that she was in on the secret, so Gretchen tried to keep up the charade. "Why would the mayor care about the floor of a building being torn down?"

"I have no idea," Chandler answered. "But it seems a little cruel, if you ask me."

"Don't you have your Advice Quilting Bee tonight?" Gretchen asked. "Maybe you could ask one of them if they know what the mayor meant."

Chandler let out a sigh and shrugged her shoulders. "I don't think I can handle them right now. I think I'll just skip it and go home."

Gretchen tried not to have a look of panic on her face. She knew the whole plan was for Chandler to go to the bee, and if she wasn't there, it would be a bust. She motioned Luann toward the back of the bakery. "You need to get a message to Myrtle that Chandler isn't planning on coming tonight!" she whispered.

"I'll send her a text message right now," Luann agreed, pulling her cell phone out of her pocket. "Grandma Myrtle loves getting text messages."

Chandler was just closing up the shop when Myrtle came barging in. "What is this I hear that you are not coming to Rosie's tonight?" Gretchen and Luann smiled and gave each other a thumbs-up.

Chandler just rubbed her forehead. She didn't have a headache, but if she had to look at Myrtle's bright orange and lime green outfit for too long she was certain one would develop. "I'm just not in the mood tonight," Chandler answered. "I'm afraid my stitches would look a mess and I'd just have to take them out anyway." Even after the events that took place two nights earlier at the winery, Chandler was still not in the mood for the entire group. She was still trying to figure out the message her father had brought to her.

"Oh, bull. Now, come on. Get your things and let's go," Myrtle said, more than a little frustrated. Seeing Chandler roll her eyes, she continued, "Don't roll your eyes at me like a teenager! Get moving!" She was sounding more like a drill sergeant.

Fine! Chandler thought. She knew when not to argue with Myrtle. She'd just keep bugging her until she went, so she might as well get it over with. She finished closing up the shop, locked the door, and followed Myrtle down to Rosie's.

When they entered the shop, Chandler noticed all the ladies were in the back standing around the quilting frame. She thought it strange, because usually they would all be sitting around eating at that time. As Myrtle pushed her toward one side of the frame, Chandler noticed there was a cover on it. *Strange,* she thought. "Why is there a cover over the quilt we started last week?" she asked looking around at everyone. "MaryAnn, why do you look like you are about to cry?" she asked, nervously. "What's wrong?" Chandler looked around and everyone was accounted for, so she knew no one had become ill, or worse.

"Oh, nothing," said MaryAnn, wiping her eye. "I have something in my eye."

Chandler looked at Rosie. "Is there a new quilt under the cover?" she asked. "We haven't even finished the other one yet, have we?"

"No, my dear," said Rosie, taking Chandler's hand. She turned to the others. "Ladies, carefully take the cover off."

Chandler watched as they gently pulled back the cloth. She couldn't believe what she was seeing. "What is this?" Chandler asked Rosie, not understanding what was going on.

"As you can see," Rosie explained, waving her hand over the quilt," this is Main Street in quilt form."

Chandler looked at the quilt, confused by what she saw. This Main Street, however, was different from the current one. Yes, she saw the fire station, hardware store, bank, Hilltop Restaurant, Rosie's, Fran's mercantile, and all the other buildings, including her bakery. But upon further inspection, Chandler also saw that the park had been revamped to include a beautiful gazebo and playground, and there were additions of two office buildings behind current storefronts, placed in such a way as to not detract from the small town charm of Main Street.

Chandler looked at Rosie, still confused, "I don't understand."

"I think there is someone here who might be able to explain it to you better than I can," Rosie said, softly.

Everyone turned toward Rosie's office when the door opened. "What? I don't understand," said Chandler again, looking around at everyone. By now she noticed that apparently many of the women had something in their eye, because there were more on the verge of crying.

Peter walked to stand beside Chandler facing the quilt. "This is the new proposal," he explained, "My proposal, and it has already been approved by the mayor. The town council will be voting to approve it tonight. They agreed to waive the public hearing, because they were all in agreement that the public would love it."

Since Chandler seemed to be at a loss for words at the moment, he continued, "We'll be investing in the town. As you can see, the park is going to be completely renovated to be a great gathering place for residents, complete with a large gazebo and new playground. With the exception of Hillary and Jack's already renovated building, the rest of the buildings previously set for demolition are going to get complete makeovers, including your bakery."

"But my landlord won't pay for that," Chandler interrupted, looking at him.

"I'll address that in a minute," Peter said with a smile, continuing. "We'll be building a pair of two-story office buildings behind the police station and the bank, with parking behind the Hilltop and the mercantile. The tax revenue from these will help to pay for the rest of the improvements."

"But how did you get the mayor to go along with this?" Chandler asked, in a bit of shock.

"Once I told him about how important the history was to the residents of Hope Springs, and that this is also an election year, he was hooked," Peter explained, smiling. "Also, we are going to be renovating the Cotton Mill and turning it into condos for sale, which will lead to more revenue to cover the cost of the work."

"So that's how you're going to fix my building?" Chandler asked, still a bit confused.

Peter smiled. "Not exactly. Apparently your landlord was thinking about selling the property. So I bought it." He smiled even bigger with a shrug.

Chandler just stared at him. "*You're* my new landlord?!"

Peter turned her so she faced him head on. "Actually, I don't think that a husband should be the landlord for his wife's business." He waited to see if he got any reaction from Chandler. She didn't move, but he could tell there was a lot of eye-wiping and sniffling going on around them. "Chandler, did you hear what I just said?"

Chandler was sure she must not have heard him correctly. "Did you really just refer to us as husband and wife?" she whispered, hopefully.

Peter could see she was going to need more visual aids here, so he got down on one knee, and pulled a little box from his jacket pocket. "Chandler Bradford, I know we've only been on two real dates, but I feel like I've known you all my life. I love you more than anything. Will you make me the happiest man alive, and marry me?" He opened the box to reveal a beautiful solitaire diamond ring.

Chandler stared at the ring. "Before I answer, I have a few questions for you."

Peter looked up at her, "Of course, ask me anything. No more lies, only truths."

"Okay," Chandler began. "First, since you now own my building, I take it the bakery is going to stay in business. That would be a very long commute for me to come from the city every day."

Peter knew where she was headed with this. "That won't be necessary. I'm planning on using one of those new office buildings for my company headquarters and keep a satellite office in the city. Since I'll be headquartered here in Hope Springs, I'll only have to go to the city occasionally."

"So, you don't mind living in Hope Springs?" she asked, feeling hopeful for the first time all week.

"Nope," he answered, "and if it means living in your cozy green house with the fuchsia door, for the rest of my life, I'm fine with that."

Chandler loved that answer. She realized that he was still on one knee, but before she gave him his answer, she had just one more question, "What happened to Cassia?" she asked, smiling. "I really don't want her moving here to work for your company."

Peter shifted to the other knee. "Not a problem because I fired her," he said, smiling. "Now if there are no more questions, may I please have an answer? My knees are going numb."

Chandler looked around at everyone again, stopping on Rosie. Rosie gave her a nod. Chandler looked back at Peter and said with a huge smile, "I love you, too, Peter. Yes, I'll marry you!"

Peter made his way to his feet and placed the ring on Chandler's finger. "I love you, Chandler Bradford, and I can't wait to see what the future holds for us."

"Aren't you gonna kiss her?" asked Myrtle loudly. Everyone laughed through tears of joy, and a few whistled as Peter gave Chandler a proper kiss.

As everyone gathered around to congratulate the newly engaged couple, MaryAnn pulled Chandler aside. "Chandler, do you remember Steven, the waiter at the winery?" she asked.

"Yes, of course," Chandler answered, looking at her strangely. "Why?"

MaryAnn pulled a piece of paper out of her sewing apron pocket, "This was given to me at the winery."

Chandler looked at her note and gave a little scream, more of delight than fright.

"What's wrong?" asked Peter, clearly worried about his bride-to-be.

Chandler looked at him through more tears and showed him the note. "That's my father's handwriting. I'd recognize it anywhere. He's giving us his blessing from heaven."

Peter hugged his bride-to-be and said a silent *thank you* toward the heavens.

Author Notes

I really enjoyed creating the lively cast of characters who live in Hope Springs, Virginia! I hope you enjoyed them as well. If you did, **please consider leaving a review.** Since I'm an independent author, I rely heavily on my readers to spread the word ☺. Also, be sure to follow me at www.jenniferskinnellquilting.com for future release dates on the next installment of the Hope Springs Romance Series. Thanks so much!

Love and Happy Reading,

Jennifer

Made in the USA
Middletown, DE
26 February 2019